Heartland
Second novel in the "New Life in Love" Trilogy

By

Teresa LaBella

This is an imprint of 4Wurdz Press
Caledonia, Nova Scotia Canada

Author's Web site www.storyteller30.com
4Wurdz Press www.4wurdz.com

Acknowledgements:
My love and sincere gratitude goes out to my talented editors – Linda Cook, Lucinda Resnick and Nancy Senn - who question my characters' motives, correct grammar, red-line typos, and keep me and the stories I create in line and on track.

I couldn't write a word without the encouragement of my biggest fan, most honest critic, best friend and love of my life. Thank you, John.

I love to connect with my readers! Feel free to contact me on Twitter, Facebook, online and by email:-

teresa.storyteller30@gmail.com

One year ago today I lost the love of my life. **The thought pierced his soul.**

His shaking hands scattered the pile of papers to the floor. His eyes saw only her. His ears heard her voice. He reached out for her but the arms that pulled her to him were empty. He fell to his knees, hugged his ribs and struggled for air between wrenching sobs delayed and suppressed since the violent collision that killed his joy.

He felt the scratch of Ivory's tongue lapping at streams of unleashed tears on his cheeks. He buried his face in her fur and wept.

Total exhaustion eventually conquered his emotional agony in the darkness of fallen night. He closed his eyes against the world without her and slept on the hardwood floor beside the vigilant Husky.

Reader reviews

"A wide variety of characters contribute to the richness of the story and the dialogue is very well written. Each character has his or her own plans and dreams – some not so clear cut, and the second half of the book takes us along on the journey to work that all out."
*..... **Karen Nortman**, author of the Frannie Shoemaker Campground mystery series.*

"I like well-written books and this is a well-written book. Coming from the Heartland I can identify with many of the characters and life in a small town. For those of us who have suffered a loss the author does a great job in helping the reader understand Darien's state of mind. It is well worth reading!"

Dedication
For my blue-eyed angels
"Ivory" and "Priya" my beloved
Gone too soon and waiting for me
at the Rainbow Bridge

Books by Teresa LaBella
Romance
Reservations
Heartland
Belonging
Tales from Heartland
Romantic Suspense
The UnMatchables Case #1: Danger Noted

Ali

Chapter 1

"Welcome to paradise, my love."

Darien McKenna gently brushed salt-and-pepper bangs from the forehead of his sleeping wife and kissed her closed eyelids. Alison Clarke McKenna smiled, stretched between the crisp white linens on the luxury hotel suite's California king-sized bed, and wrapped slender arms around his neck. "Mmmm," she sighed and lifted her head above the mound of pillows to kiss him. "Come back to bed and make love."

Darien laughed low and slid the aquamarine bikini in his hand between his bare chest and the sheet that covered hers. "Let's go for a swim first."

She opened her eyes and lay back to admire him. After eight years together and seven years of marriage, she still could not believe this tall, dark and indescribably handsome man born the same year she had graduated from college was her husband. In the soft glow of the bedside lamp, his raven black hair showed no hint of the steel grey color of his eyes. He'd taken care not to let the love of food and wine that led him to a career as an executive chef add unwanted inches to his waistline. The swim trunks he wore clung to lean abs and muscular thighs and his broad shoulders carried arms symmetrically sculpted. "In the dark?" she protested.

He straightened, strolled to the suite's compact kitchenette, and poured two steaming cups of dark roast Kona blend from the carafe under the sputtering coffee maker. A thin sliver of approaching daylight poked through the divide in the drapes that covered the sliding door portal leading to a lanai overlooking Waikiki beach. "Not for long. The sun will be coming up over Diamond Head soon." He went to her and offered the cup clutched in his strong and steady hand.

"I realize it's been a long time since we took one," she said between sips of coffee. "But aren't we meant to sleep in when on vacation?"

He smiled and bent to kiss her again. "Ali, we have slept in. It's after nine in New York."

"You always have been an early riser."

"Twenty years in a kitchen will do that to you."

"But you haven't been an executive chef for seven years."

He shrugged and sat on the bed. "I guess it's a tough habit for me to break."

She finished her coffee, set the cup on the bedside table, and rested her cheek on a hand propped up by her bent arm and elbow. "Do you ever regret leaving Chez Nous?"

He reached out and caressed the lovely face he'd fallen in love with at first sight over bruschetta he'd served her at a charity gala to help the hungry of New York. Those chocolate brown eyes had haunted him until he found her. "The hours were brutal and too many away from you."

"You could have bought a restaurant and been your own boss."

"I am my own boss. And I like helping owners and chefs open restaurants. Every consult is a new and different challenge with its own rewards."

She nodded. "I feel the same about every one of my clients. I loved the rush of reporting and editing a daily newspaper. But the less exciting finance and personnel management part of owning a media consulting business is worth it, especially since I set my own hours." She tossed off the sheets that covered her naked body, as beautiful to him as the first time they'd made love, and slipped the bikini top straps over her slender shoulders. "OK. I'll take you up on that pre-dawn dip."

Darien stripped off his swim trunks and cupped her breasts in his hands before the filmy material could cover them. "On second thought, let's go with your idea," he said, and covered her lips and body with his.

Ali studied the lunch menu in her hands through the lenses of the red-rimmed eyeglasses on her nose and sighed. "I have no idea what to order." The words loaded with vowels and consonants in unusual pairings described native Hawaiian daily specials totally foreign to her.

"We always order the pupu platter." Ali's cousin Patrice Lacey and her husband Dan hadn't bothered to look at the single page menu at rest on their white paper placemats. "It's the best way to sample what the islands have to offer," she explained.

"We found that out the hard way the first time we came over with a tour group," Dan said and rolled his eyes. "Never again!" The big man with the unrestrained mop of grey hair and ever-present grin leaned toward Darien across the wooden tabletop blemished by years of the customers served. "Please tell me you didn't try the so-called native food at that Waikiki tourist trap."

"Not on your life," Darien said. "All we've had so far is standard room service fare and fresh produce from the market near Chinatown."

"Well, this is the place to get genuine native cuisine," Dan said. "We found it on our return trip to Honolulu and come back every time."

"How often do you visit?" Ali asked.

"After we bought the north shore condo and Dan retired, we started booking a flight every two or three months," Patrice answered. "Take a nap on the plane from San Francisco and we're here in no time at all."

"How can you take that much time off from work?" Ali asked.

Patrice smiled. "I only work two or three days a week when I want to."

"Are you ready to order?" The petite young waitress with almond-shaped eyes and a smile to match her cheerful greeting stood at the end of the table between Darien and Dan.

"I'd like a few minutes more, please," Ali responded.

"Take your time." The waitress turned away to check on another table of guests nearby.

"I don't eat meat but I do like seafood," Ali explained.

"Then you probably won't want Spam," Patrice teased her cousin.

Ali's eyebrows disappeared under her bangs. "Excuse me? Are you referring to that disgusting mystery meat packed in gelatin?"

"Hawaiians like Spam," Dan said. "It's almost as common here as poi."

"What's poi?" Ali asked.

"Taro," Darien answered. "It's a type of tropical tuber plant."

"Is it good?" Ali asked.

"It's an acquired taste," Patrice said. "The first time I had it, I couldn't even swallow it. But then I held my nose and tried it here. Now I really like it."

The waitress returned with her pad and pencil ready. "Still deciding?"

"How about three pupu platters and whatever you'd recommend for our non-meat eater who likes a good plate of seafood," Dan said and nodded in Ali's direction.

"I suggest the Opakapaka Pualoa."

Darien's expert eye scanned the menu and description of the entrée mentioned. "Good choice," he confirmed and handed his and Ali's menu to the waitress.

"Wait a minute," Ali protested. "What did I just order?"

"Red snapper with ginger, cilantro, onions, and a sauce I want to taste," he confirmed.

"Fine," she said. "With a side order of poi, please," she told the waitress.

After lunch had been served and enjoyed and the empty plates cleared, the couples lingered over cups of coffee and slices of Kona lime pie.

Patrice licked her lips and sighed with pleasure. "I don't know why this tastes so much better than plain old key lime pie."

"Maybe it's the place," Dan observed and ate his last bit of crumbled crust.

"It's probably the combination of coconut and sour cream," Darien commented.

Patrice flipped thick ash blonde and silver-streaked hair over sun-kissed shoulders and winked a pale blue eye at him. "No ingredient gets past the former chef."

"How's life been out of the kitchen?" Dan asked.

"I'm still in the kitchen," Darien responded. "I just don't stay on after the opening."

"That's got to be a lot less stress," Dan said.

"Yes and no. True, I can walk away. But there are anxious moments and hot words before the doors open."

"You've held up well over the years, cousin," Patrice remarked to Ali. "I see just a few more grey hairs since I was your matron of honor. How long ago was that?"

"Seven years last August and no sign of an itch," she said and squeezed Darien's hand. "You haven't aged at all, Patrice."

"Dan deserves some of the credit. He convinced me that I needed to revisit my priorities. When he retired, I realized less work and more play seemed like a lot more fun. My plan is to drop out of the grind altogether so we can move here for good next fall."

"Really? But you're only 62."

"And so are you, cousin. You're seven months older than me, so you'll be 63 on Christmas Eve. Tell me, when was the last time before this week that the two of you got away from work and New York? Long weekends don't count."

Ali and Darien looked at other. "Well, we, no, I think it was, didn't we go to?" they stammered. Ali answered for them both. "I honestly don't remember."

"Your honeymoon in Paris, perhaps?" Patrice asked. They nodded. "Shame on you!"

Dan shook his head. "Life is way too short to spend so much of it making money."

"Money you don't really need," Patrice added, "and time is a commodity you cannot buy. Think about it. If you both stopped working tomorrow, would you be out on the street?"

Ali laughed. "Of course not."

"So how drastically would your life and lifestyles change? Other than having more time to enjoy it and each other?"

Darien's arm circled Ali's shoulders. "Interesting question," he said.

Dan signaled the waitress. "How about we continue this conversation at the condo?"

"Great idea, hon," Patrice chimed in. "It's a two hour plus drive from Waikiki. Why not grab what you need from the hotel and spend the night? Bring swimsuits." She winked again. "But forget the pajamas."

The scenic drive up Kamehameha Highway past Kaneohe Bay ended in the driveway of Dan and Patrice's modest two-bedroom piece of real estate in paradise. Patrice surprised her guests with bottles of French chardonnay and Chilean merlot.

"I thought only California wine was worthy enough to grace your table," Ali remarked.

"Dan blindsided me at dinner one night with a full carafe and no bottle." Patrice poured four glasses of chilled golden fermented grapes grown and bottled at a vineyard on the other side of the world. "I still prefer the Napa or Sonoma Valley vintage. But variety is the spice of life, or so I'm told." She smiled at her husband.

Dan clapped Darien on the shoulder and handed him his glass. "My grill may not be as grand as that monster on your rooftop garden in Brooklyn. But here you can flip burgers or sear fresh seafood and hear the ocean."

"After you," Darien said and followed Dan through the sliding glass entryway to the outdoor lanai.

Patrice sat back against the overstuffed sofa splashed with fabric printed in tropical green, mauve and yellow and smiled at her cousin. "How's life, love and the pursuit of marital sanity?"

Ali laughed, propped her bare feet up on the sofa's matching footstool and wiggled her pedicured toes. "Life can be crazy. But the love more than makes up for it and Darien keeps me sane."

"I am so happy you're living your happily ever after." Patrice drank the last of her wine and poured more. "I really think the two of you should retire sooner rather than too later."

"You make it sound as though we've got one foot in the grave. We're not that old, Patrice. And need I remind you Darien is much younger."

"But he's been working in a kitchen since he was 16. And you've been busting your pretty little butt for over 40 years. You both deserve to turn the page and write the next chapters of your life together as you want to live it."

"You're not going to get off this topic, are you?"

Patrice topped up Ali's glass of wine. "Just tell me you'll think about it."

Ali touched the rim of her full glass to the half-empty glass in Patrice's hand. "I promise you that I will take it under advisement," she said.

Dan and Darien sat side-by-side in chaise lounges, listened to the sound of the waves and watched for the "green flash" of sunset as day slipped smoothly into silky island night.

"I don't suppose you have sesame oil and lime juice for those ahi steaks?" Darien asked.

"Oil, sesame seeds and fresh limes."

"Even better." Darien ignited the propane and prepared the grill while Dan retrieved and returned with the main course, plates, utensils and all needed ingredients from the kitchen.

"Patrice promised to stop drinking wine long enough to make a salad," Dan assured Darien, who laughed and plopped seasoned tuna onto the hot grate.

"Hey, thanks for inviting us to stay the night," Darien said. "Even a hotel suite gets old real fast."

"That's the reason why Patrice and I decided to buy this place. We like the home away from home feel. And the private beach sealed the deal."

Darien's eyebrows arched. "Beach front came with the property?"

"Yeah. It's not much, but it's ours. We'll walk down and go for a swim in the morning."

Darien sighed. "Man, this is heaven. If Ali and I owned a home here, I'm not sure we would ever leave."

"It gets tougher every time, believe me. Patrice and I are flying home to San Francisco the day after tomorrow. But we're planning to come back right after the holidays." Dan snapped his fingers and his expression brightened with an idea. "How long are you and Ali staying in the islands?"

"A couple more weeks. We've got reservations on Maui next week and the Big Island the week after."

"Why don't you check out of the hotel in Waikiki and stay here while you're on Oahu?"

"That's a very generous offer."

"Hey, you're family. Besides, why let the place sit empty?"

Ali slid naked between cool linens that covered the queen-sized guest room bed. Her head swirled with wine and the delicious memory of fresh fish grilled to perfection and crisp mixed greens dressed in Darien's own vinaigrette. She could hear her husband in the hallway on the other side of the closed door thanking their hosts for giving them the spare key to their condo. She smiled at the turn of the doorknob and soft click that closed them in. Darien moved toward her in moonlight filtered through window-dressing sheers that fluttered in the island breeze. She took his hand and guided his open palm under the sheet and over her breast. "No pajamas," she whispered and began to unbutton his shirt.

"Didn't pack any," he whispered back and dropped discarded shorts and briefs to the floor.

Two weeks later, the couple spent their last morning in paradise sipping coffee on the condo lanai as the sky blushed pink with the first rays of dawn.

"Sorry I woke you so early, my love. But I'm selfish." Darien turned and leaned his back against the railing. "I wanted to enjoy every minute of vacation we have left."

Ali circled his waist with her arm and snuggled against him. "I suppose we do need to ease back into Eastern time." She tilted her head back and smiled up at him. Her chocolate brown eyes reflected the gathering gold of tropical daylight. "Are you sorry we skipped Maui and the Big Island?"

"Anywhere I am with you is where I want to be. We can take in Haleakala and the volcanoes next time." Her kiss tasted of coffee and desire and he parted her lips with his tongue for more. He set down his cup, scooped her into his arms and carried her through the open lanai doors. She was surprised when he set her back on her feet and tossed her a towel.

"Let's go down to the beach one last time," he said, dropped his robe on the bed, pulled on his swim trunks and grabbed a towel of his own.

She shook her head. "You still surprise me," she said and exchanged the robe for her bikini.

"I always will," he answered. He took her hand to walk the sloping path that led to golden sand and blue water. They stayed connected to each other as gentle waves lapped at the flip-flops on their feet, rolled in against their thighs and splashed over Ali's breasts. Darien lifted her up and she held on, her arms around his neck, her legs locked around his waist. He kissed the salt water from her neck and lips. His fingers burrowed beneath the bikini to find her sweet spot. He fondled, caressed and pressed the quivering, throbbing mound with his thumb, sank and wriggled exploring fingers in the wet warmth within her. Ali dug her fingernails into his back and cried out as each wave of shivering, shimmering delight crested, flowed, receded, and washed over her again.

He waded out of the Pacific with the love of his life writhing in his arms and laid her beauty on the sand. The bikini's front clasp slipped open and away in his hands. His lips and tongue feasted on her bared breasts and raised nipples and he pulled at the knotted string above her hip.

"Darien!" Ali gasped. "We are not alone on this island!"

Every fantasy he'd conjured in his wildest dreams lay beneath him. Her face flushed like flame, her full lips luscious red as cabernet, her wide brown eyes glinting like chocolate diamonds in the slanted shafts of advancing sunlight. He loved every strand of ocean-washed hair, every sensuous curve, the lingering scent of her favorite lilac fragrance, her musical laugh, graceful walk, brilliant mind and generous heart. He loved her and longed to live this realized fantasy forever.

"Ali, my love, my life. Right here, right now, this island is ours alone." He cradled her lovely face in his hands and kissed her again and again. Softly, slowly, deeply. "I love you," he whispered. "I'll love you forever." He pulled the second knot free.

"I love you," she whispered back. Her hands pushed back fabric and slid the swim trunks over his hips and pelvis. Her china doll delicate hands stroked the hard male part of him. She raised her knees, opened her legs, and guided him in. He groaned and thrust the full of him deep within her in natural rhythm with the ocean waves, driving them both to shouts of joy in the island morning.

Chapter 2

Winter's first snow dusted the endless ribbons of city concrete and remnants of autumn in New York. Darien guided another owner and chef through long frantic days leading up to a scheduled opening on New Year's Eve. Ali coached clients, negotiated contracts and poured over Clarke Media Consultants financials with veteran associate Kenny Wong. They huddled over the conference table for a third consecutive day of year-end number crunching. Laptop computers, piles of sorted paper and empty coffee cups littered the conference table they huddled over in her Brooklyn office on Water Street.

Ali ruffled through the stack of invoices and receipts and sighed. "So much for the paperless office." She sat back and swiveled her chair away from the fiscal mayhem. "This gets more tedious every year."

Kenny pulled a white handkerchief from his pants pocket and wiped eyeglass lenses rimmed by silver frames. "On the contrary, I think it gets easier."

"Then maybe you should take over the business," she said.

Kenny held his glasses up to the light overhead and checked for smudges. "I'd love to. But then what would you do?"

"Spend glorious days of uninterrupted bliss with my husband."

Kenny laughed. "I doubt that Darien is ready for the old rocking chair."

"That depends on where the rocking chair is. A villa in Tuscany. A chalet at Innsbruck. A veranda in Auckland. "

"OK, OK, I get where you're going with this." Kenny patted the front of the white shirt above his belt. "I'm also getting hungry."

"I thought you might be." Mimi Teague appeared from the outer office carrying white paper bags imprinted with the name of the nearby Chinese restaurant owned and staffed by Kenny's family. The four-inch heels on ankle boots intended to make the petite woman look taller tapped with each step across the hardwood floor. She placed the bags at the center of the table and pulled gloves from hands a shade lighter than her brown wool coat. "I hope you don't mind home-cooked food. But I just had to have your sister's Szechwan shrimp."

"Mimi, you're a life saver." Kenny took her coat and pulled out a chair at the conference table. His hands, equally familiar with serving plates of food as entering data on spread sheets, dipped into the bags that yielded containers of steamed rice and vegetables, spicy shrimp, Mongolian beef and chopsticks wrapped in paper.

"Thank you, Mimi." Ali slid the paper wrapper off her chopsticks and lifted a thin slice of green pepper from her container. "Is Alex home for Christmas break?"

"He got in late last night." Mimi stirred shrimp into rice and grinned at the woman who had hired her when no one else would. "His ride to Houston was delayed by finals and he missed his flight out. Then weather grounded the plane in Atlanta. Poor baby was so tired. He'll probably sleep all day."

"At least he'll be closer to home next year," Kenny said between bites of beef.

Mimi's face shone with pride for her only son, a semester away from graduation at Texas A&M. "Imagine. My boy at Yale."

"Impressive," Kenny commented. "But not cheap."

"He'll be working on campus and the scholarship helps," Mimi explained. "He got a grant to cover the rest."

"Yeah, I know. It's on the books," Kenny said.

Mimi looked puzzled. "What do you mean?"

Kenny glanced at their boss and bit his lip. "Oops. My bad."

"It's OK, Kenny," Ali assured him. "Yale accepts grants from employers of student's parents," Ali told Mimi.

Mimi blinked. "I-I don't know what to say," she stammered. "Thank you isn't enough."

"Mimi, you've helped me keep this business going for 20 years. I thank you by investing in Alex. I can open the door. It's up to him to step through it."

"Happy Birthday, Ali!" David Dupuis called through the open doorway of Ali and Darien's top floor apartment. Tufts of blonde hair poked out from under the green felt elf's hat tipped with a silver bell that he wore every holiday season, His hands, protected by hot pads, held the traditional pot of oyster stew.

"And Merry Christmas." David's dark-haired partner Jayson Denning handed Darien a bottle of golden chardonnay.

Darien read the label and smiled. "Great choice. Let's pop the cork and get this party started."

"Looks like you already have, love." David set the pot of stew on the dining room table next to the red roses and white lilacs arrangement he'd sent his longtime landlord, employer and best friend and picked up an uncorked bottle of pinot grigio.

Ali's grin, flushed cheeks and half-empty wine glass had given her away. "I'm allowed." She patted the cushion beside her on the butter-colored leather sectional near the dancing flames of the bio-fueled fireplace.

"Don't get comfortable," Darien warned. "I could use some help."

"Yes, Chef. " David joined Darien at the large island prep area that defined and separated the kitchen from the apartment's open concept dining and living spaces. His expert hands and food stylist attention to detail plated and garnished smoked salmon, iced oysters on the half shell and arranged chilled jumbo shrimp into a perfect horseshoe.

"What's this?" Jayson followed the scent puffing from a pot on the six-burner stovetop.

"French onion soup for us meat lovers," Darien said over his shoulder as he sliced a steaming loaf of freshly baked sour dough bread.

Jayson breathed in the pungent aroma of simmering onions, beef, broth and garlic and sighed in anticipation. "Thank you," he said. "Now I can avoid all the oysters this Christmas."

David stopped shucking and pointed the oyster knife at his partner. "I know you won't touch raw oysters. But I thought you liked my oyster stew."

Jayson raised his hands in a gesture of apology. "I've tried to tell you but I didn't want to hurt your feelings."

"Oh, really." David put down the knife and wiped his hands on a kitchen towel. "Do tell what else I make that you'd rather not eat."

Ali appeared between them, a full glass of chardonnay in each hand. "Not today, boys," she scolded them. "This is my day. I love you both and you love each other. So drink, kiss, make up and shut up."

Red velvet cake layered with creamy icing and glasses of dry white wine to cleanse the sweet dessert from their palates topped off Ali's birthday dinner. The evening passed in the comfort and joy of a Christmas gift exchange between friends, shared plans for the next day and memories of holidays past.

Darien held his wife close and squeezed her shoulder. "Ali started Christmas shopping before we went to Hawaii and hasn't stopped since. There are so many packages in our home office I haven't been able to get through the obstacle course to my desk since we got back."
Jayson pointed at the piles of wrapped gifts under and around the twinkling tree in the corner. "You mean there's more than what's under the tree?"

"Those are for us to open tomorrow morning and for Mimi and Kenny to take home to their families after Christmas," Ali said. "The gifts in the home office go with us tomorrow to Jack and Beth's in Montclair."

"You aren't having Christmas at your parents' place?" David asked Darien.

"The family got too big for the row house in Hoboken so we moved it to my brother and sister-in-law's place this year. My niece's boyfriend and his parents and her roommate from college will be there and my nephew invited a classmate who apparently doesn't have the best home life. Beth's sister Julia got engaged and she's bringing her fiancé. But I'm not sure if they're staying for dinner."

"Sounds like Christmas at the Dennings," David remarked. "There are so many aunts, uncles, cousins and various other extended family members plugging up his folks' apartment in Queens it is standing room only all day long."

"Oh, I almost forgot to tell you," Jayson interrupted. "My sister got engaged today. "Mom was so excited when she called that she couldn't talk. Dad took the phone away from her to tell me. He's pretty happy, too."

Ali raised her nearly-empty wine glass. "Alla famiglia" she said, quoting the closing line from *Moonstruck,* the cinematic romance that held a place of honor in the extensive collection of film aficionados Ali and Darien. "Love changes everything."

"It sure did for you and me, Ali," David said. "We haven't had Christmas dinner at Wong's since we started cohabitating with our significant others. But here we are in the same spot we were on Christmas Eve the week before you moved in, Darien," David said. "As I recall, you scooped up Ali, kicked poor old Max out of the bedroom and slammed the French doors in our faces. I took Max home with me that night." He sighed at the memory. "I sure miss that shelter mutt. He was a great dog."

Jayson frowned at David. "Well. I guess I know where I stand. The humane society is closed tomorrow. But I'm sure we could find you a suitable roommate the day after."

David brightened, apparently missing the point. "That's a great idea! We'll adopt a dog on my birthday after we go to city hall."

"Why do we need to go to city hall?" Jayson asked. "I'm pretty sure we can get a dog license at the shelter."

"But we can't get a marriage license there." David took his partner's hands in his. "Maybe it's your sister's news or spending a delightful evening with the most happily married couple I know. I want that for us, Jayson. I want us to be married."

Jayson's jaw dropped open and tears filled his ocean-green eyes. "You do? So do I," he said.

Ali brushed away her tears and snuggled against Darien. "This is the best birthday ever!" she said.

Chapter 3

Darien tossed his coat on the sectional, dropped into its cushions and rubbed his throbbing temples with the heels of his palms. "I have never come so close to walking off a job," he told his wife.

"I feel your pain, love" she said and sat beside him. "I'm about to tear up a contract and tell a client to find another firm."

"You go first," they said together and each smiled for the first time that day.

"I'm tired of ticking off my check list of complaints," he said. "Tell me yours."

Ali's description of a diva with questionable talent versus a clueless corporate representative in a suit and crooked bow tie bobbing under a very pronounced Adam's apple released waves of pent up frustration and laughter from her husband. "Thanks honey," he said and kissed her. "I really needed that."

"Your turn," she said and nestled under his arm against his chest.

"Well." He took a deep breath and relayed the relentless demands of a restaurant owner pushing to open his upper West Side restaurant by Valentine's Day. "He changes his mind by the hour and is driving me and the construction crew crazy. He can't seem to decide on a design or a menu. And to make matters worse, he's hired an exec with a shitload of paper training but not much else. The guy has no idea what he's doing. He's a total idiot in a kitchen."

"Valentine's Day is less than two weeks away," Ali observed. "Will the restaurant be ready?"

Darien shrugged his shoulders. "I honestly don't know. But I always finish what I start. The beauty of consulting is I'll stay until the doors open and walk away."

Darien visited Myron, the jeweler who had crafted Ali's engagement ring, and picked up the heart-shaped ruby pendant set in 18-carat white gold by the aging artist. He cruised Manhattan's markets for ingredients he would combine to create three courses of gastronomic delight brought to a table dressed with roses and illuminated by quivering candlelight. The champagne would chill in a silver bucket by the swirling, soothing water in the jetted tub of their master suite. He'd wrap her in a warm towel and carry her to their bed where he'd admire her beauty, caress her to climax, dive in to her, release with her and fill only her as long as they both shall live.

He planned to hit the newly opened restaurant's front doors at four in the afternoon on Valentine's Day and be in the back of a cab crossing the Brooklyn Bridge before five. He rolled up the sleeve of his borrowed chef coat, checked his watch, and swore under his breath at six. The red-faced, frantic exec hired by the owner had worked the line in panicked desperation, trying to prep chateaubriand for the ovens. Darien took over the kitchen, demoted the equally inept sous chef, and promoted the more level-headed line cook.

He called and left a voice mail message for Ali at 6:30. "Sorry, sweetheart, I'm stuck at the restaurant. I'll be home as soon as I can."

He left another message at 8. "We're snowed again here. Where are you?" He finally reached her at 9:30.

"I just got in," she said. "What happened?"

"The idiot exec had a meltdown. Nothing would have gone out of this kitchen if I hadn't stayed. The owner has been kissing my ass since seven."

Ali laughed. "Any idea when I may expect to see your well-kissed gorgeous ass?"

"There could be a full moon by midnight," he joked. He took his wife in his arms and kissed her at 11:58.

Ali slipped away from her sleeping husband at seven thirty the next morning and left a message directing Mimi to cancel her appointments through noon. She set their table for two as she had the morning after they'd first made love, poured orange juice and prepared a pile of toast. She was scrambling eggs when he came up behind her and wrapped his arms around her waist.

"You're not wearing my shirt," he said and nuzzled her neck.

"It wasn't on the floor."

"I'll gladly get one from the closet."

"Why?" She turned in his arms and opened her robe. The slippery silk dropped from her naked shoulders to the floor. "I turned up the heat."

"You sure did." He kissed her, lips to breasts, knelt in front of her, caressed the curves of her calves and thighs with his palms and cradled her heat in his hands. His lips closed over her and his tongue flicked and probed her until her knees softened. He lifted her onto the smooth counter, parted her legs and savored the juices of their lovemaking. She leaned her head back against the upper cupboards, curled her fingers around the handles within reach and moaned his name again and again as he sipped her nectar. He dropped and spread the soft fabric of his robe onto the floor.

"Oh, my beautiful love." He took her in his arms, lay her on his robe and entered her, slowly, methodically, prolonging their pleasure, his palms pressed against the hardwood, his hips moving in circular motions. She dug her heels into the floor and matched his movements. Her hands gripped his shoulders, her lips urged him on.

"Ali…I can't…"

"Then don't." She thrust her hips to his and he drove full into her, unleashing the power of passion shared.

Darien tossed out the cold eggs and toast, showered, dressed and made omelets while Ali got ready for her day in the office. He retrieved the ruby heart pendant he'd intended to give her the day before and set the unopened box on her plate at the table.

"What's this?" she asked, opened the box and gasped. "Oh, Darien. It's beautiful. Here," she said and handed him the box. "Put it on me, please."

He chuckled and fastened the clasp. "That's a much different response than the one I got when I proposed."

She turned back to him and his heart leapt at the look of pure love in her lovely brown eyes. She slipped the diamond solitaire away from her wedding band and handed it to him. "Ask me again," she said.

Darien got down on one knee as he had in the dining room at Chez Nous on Valentine's Day eight years before. "Alison, would you marry me again?"

She smiled and caressed his cheek with her fingertips. "Yes, Darien. I will forever and always be your wife."

Darien prepared their Valentine's Day feast on February the fifteenth. They laughed about the wilting roses and fed each other spoonfuls of chocolate soufflé by candlelight. Ali took a rain check on champagne and the jetted tub in favor of an early night embrace beneath crisp sheets and a fluffy down comforter.

Darien stroked her hair and kissed her forehead. "You never did tell me why you were so late getting home last night."

"I spent hours mediating a dispute between a legend in her own mind diva and the corporate suit with the ugly neck and bow tie. Turns out his boss didn't like her choice of lipstick and nail color."

"Are you kidding me?"

"I wish I were. All she had to do was agree to swap deep purple for gaudy pink."

He groaned. "I'm tired of wasting our life and time on these people. Maybe Patrice and Dan have the right idea."

"Are you suggesting we retire?"

"I'm way past the suggestion stage. Ali, I think we should do it."

"When?"

"The sooner the better. If I don't take on any more jobs, I'll finish up what's on my plate by June."

"I can't close down the firm that soon. I've got clients to represent and Mimi and Kenny to consider."

"Kenny already owns a piece of the business, right?"

"Yes."

"So what would it take to sell an equal portion to Mimi?"

"I don't know her financial comfort level."

"Honey, you've told me Kenny is a master at manipulating the numbers to make things work. What could it hurt to ask them, measure their level of interest?" He frowned when she giggled. "I'm serious about this."

"I know you are, my love. But your metaphors are all about food. Finish what's on your plate. A piece of the business. An equal portion. Measure their level of interest." She kissed his lips and lightly nibbled his neck. "Always the chef. Are you sure you want to give that up?"

"Absolutely."

Darien hesitated when his sous chef from Chez Nous called the next day to make him an offer Eric Lanahan was certain his former boss couldn't refuse.

"C'mon, Chef," pleaded the new owner of the restaurant on the third floor of the Time Warner Building where the two men had worked side-by-side for seven years. "I really need your help turning this place around. The kitchen needs an upgrade, the décor is tired and the menu is atrocious. I know we could bring it back even better than before. It would be like old times. What do you say?"

"I don't know, man. Don't get me wrong, I'm tempted. It's just that Ali and I are considering other options right now."

"OK, I understand. God knows Andrea and I spent a lot of sleepless nights hashing out the pros and cons of owning a restaurant after we got the kids to bed. Talk it over. But you know I won't take no for an answer."

Darien laughed. "I'll let you know by the end of the week."

Ali trotted up three flights of stairs from her office to home at the end of a long work day, invigorated at the certainty of her decision and giddy with the possibilities. Darien heard her quick footsteps and opened the front door as her fingers fumbled with the keys.

"Something wrong, sweetheart?" he asked.

She stood on tiptoe, kissed his lips, and melted into his arms. "Everything is so right!"

He breathed in her familiar scent of lilacs and kissed the top of her head. "Yes, it is."

"Let's do it," she said.

"Whatever you say."

He picked her up, kicked the front door closed, and carried her through the open French doors to their bedroom and bed. He smothered her giggles with kisses, unbuttoned her blouse and burrowed his fingers under her lace bra. She pulled the tucked shirt from his unbelted pants and drew sensual circular patterns on his flesh with her fingernails. He nibbled her raised nipples through the lace and kissed a trail to the slacks he unzipped. She opened his jeans and stroked his pulsing sex with both hands. He peeled back each layer between them, kissed every uncovered part of her and whispered his love for her. She held on to him as he entered her and cried out in pleasure at the crest of shuddering climax.

"Darien, my gorgeous love." She lay in his arms, her naked body a perfect fit with his. Uncovered, the lingering heat of their lovemaking warmed them. "That was wonderful but not exactly what I meant when I said let's do it."

"I'm not entirely surprised. But we did enjoy the diversion."

She snuggled closer against him. "We certainly did."

"What did you have in mind, my love?"

"I talked to Mimi and Kenny today about taking over the business."

"And?"

"It's not a totally done deal. There are a lot of details to work out. But we came up with a solid plan. I could retire by our anniversary." She moved in his arms and looked up at him. "What do you think?"

"That would give me time to work with Eric. You remember Eric, my sous chef?" Ali nodded. "He quit his exec job in Lower Midtown and bought Chez Nous. He called today and asked me to help him out."

"What a perfect way to end your career," she said.

"And begin our new life," he agreed.

"Let's do it!" they said together.

Chapter 4

Darien's steel grey eyes scanned the work stations in the kitchen he'd once commanded. Every appliance, utensil and smooth surface gleamed. Buzz between newly-hired prep and line cooks, sous chef and wait staff rose from the refreshed dining room. Darien strode across the polished travertine tile to where Eric huddled over the menu and inventory checklist with the exec Darien had recommended and recruited. He took one last long look through the floor to ceiling windows overlooking Columbus Circle and Central Park and smiled at the memories. He had sharpened his culinary skills and earned a Michelin star in this restaurant's kitchen, wooed and proposed to the love of his life in its dining room.

"Well, that about does it. We're as ready as we'll ever be." Eric grinned at his former boss, now colleague and friend. He stuck out his hand. "Thanks, Chef."

Darien grinned back and shook Eric's hand. "My pleasure."

"So, what's next?"

"Paris, Europe and whatever exotic places grab our fancy. I bought open-date return plane tickets for Ali and me. We leave the day after tomorrow."

"I envy you, man. Your adventure is just beginning."

"So is yours, my friend."

Darien came home to candlelight and Indian take-out from the Brooklyn restaurant the couple had ordered from the day Darien moved in.

"Beer or wine?" Ali asked her husband.

"Chardonnay," he answered."

Ali laughed. "You remembered."

"I remember every precious moment with you, my love," he said and touched her glass with his.

"Here's to making more memories and more love," she said.

"In faraway places," he responded, and handed her the travel agent's itinerary.

"What's this? Our second honeymoon in Paris?"

"And beyond." He smiled at her squeal and wide-eyed delight. "The sky is literally the limit and the world is ours to explore."

They walked hand-in-hand to the riverfront after dinner. The sky over Manhattan blazed brilliant orange against cool streaks of turquoise blue in the sultry summer evening. Ali stopped in front of a newly-installed bench, squeezed his hand and pointed toward their feet. The paver below memorialized "Max," the barrel-chested shepherd mix mutt they had loved to his last breath taken in their arms. Tears came to Darien's eyes and a smile to his lips when he read the gold letter message engraved on the plaque centered on the bench backrest.

From your brown-eyed girl
All my love
Ali

"I thought we needed a place to watch the world go by in our golden years," she said.

"With a dog at our feet," he replied.

"Rescued from the animal shelter where I adopted Max."

He took her in his arms and kissed the top of her head where the center part met bangs. "Absolutely."

Darien stuffed bare necessities in a mid-sized suitcase on wheels while Ali slid selected papers in a black leather briefcase for her last day at the helm of Clarke Media Consultants.

"That should do it," he said and zipped the case closed.

"Is that all you're going to take?" she asked.

"Yup."

"But we're going to be away for weeks."

"More like months." He patted the front pants pocket where he kept his wallet. "No point in hauling a lot of stuff around when we can buy what we need as we go."

She considered his plan, nodded and smiled. "Point taken," she said and pulled a suitcase of equal size and function from her closet. She opened the case and laughed. "I haven't used this since I moved to New York." She lifted the paperback book from inside the suitcase, turned it over in her hands, and opened the pages at the bookmark.

Darien spotted the book's title over her shoulder and grinned. "Romeo and Juliet. You told me you'd memorized the dialogue."

"From Zefferelli's film, not the entire play."

He scanned the words on the page, grimaced and whistled. "This is familiar territory for my brother the English major."

She kissed his cheek and handed him the book. "The words come to life when read out loud."

He took the book from her and bowed. "And where should I begin, my lady?"

Ali giggled. "At the top of the page, my lord."

He faked the need to clear his throat and held the book at arm's length. "Ah, dear Juliet, why art thou yet so fair? Shall I believe that unsubstantial death is amorous, and that the lean abhorred monster keeps thee here in dark to be his paramour? For fear of that, I still will stay with thee and never from this palace of dim night depart again. Here, here will I remain with worms that are thy chambermaids." He closed the book and frowned. "Yuck!"

They collapsed in laughter, tumbled onto their bed, and made love in the gentle twilight of another fading day.

Chapter 5

Darien watched his wife dress for her last day at work. "What's on your agenda today?"

"Not much. Clean out my desk and laptop this morning and drive out to Long Island this afternoon to visit my last client who was also by no coincidence my very first client."

"Why don't you have lunch with Jack and me? We could go somewhere other than the pub in Midtown."

She smiled, touched his sleeve and damn if he didn't feel the same tingle as that first time in Central Park. "Better stick with tradition."

"In all these months and years of Wednesdays, you've never had lunch with us."

"I respected your time with your brother. I didn't want to intrude."

"OK, I'll make you a deal. We'll all meet at the usual place. I'll buy you a beer and you can take a cab to Long Island."

She laughed and kissed him. "I'll skip the beer and drive myself so I can get home to you sooner."

Jack was waiting for Darien at the pub's front window two-top round table.

"We gotta switch to a four-top today," Darien said. "I invited Ali to join us." On cue, the door to the pub opened and Ali stepped through it. "Hi, sweetheart." She stood on tiptoe and kissed her husband.

Jack pretended to pout. "What about the guy holding a beer and the menus?"

She laughed, gave him a hug and settled into a chair at the only open table across from the bar and next to the wall. "How have you been, Jack? And how are Beth and the kids? Seems like ages since we've been to Montclair."

"Can't complain. Life is good. I've got my usual class load at Hoboken High this fall. Beth will be teaching first grade. Nathan starts high school in a couple weeks. He's trying to act like it's no big deal. But I know my son and he's nervous. Hannah finally declared math as her major at NYU."

"Interesting choice," Ali commented.

"Not really. She's always made straight A's in math with some help from Evan, her whiz kid high school sweetheart. He got a full ride to MIT. Nice kid. Good manners."

"Any progress on the great American novel?" his brother teased.

"For your information, smartass, I'm working on chapter four."

They ate their lunch in a flurry of exchanged family news and travel plans. Jack and Darien raised glasses of beer in salute to Ali's career accomplishments. Ali finished her Coke. "I haven't had one of those in years," she said.

"May you enjoy many more in Singapore or wherever else your plane touches down," Jack said.

Ali laughed. "With that stellar attempt at a poetic ending, I will take my leave."

"Let me settle up and I'll walk you to the car," Darien said.

"It's on me," Jack said and signaled the waitress for their bill.

"Thanks, man. I'll call you tomorrow before we leave."

"Damn straight you will," Jack said and winked at his sister-in-law.

The couple walked hand-in-hand to the parking structure where their journey began in the front seat of Ali's Mercedes. "I had a lot less gray in my hair and fewer wrinkles then," she said. "And my clothes were a size smaller. I guess that's the price I paid for falling in love with a chef."

He smiled, took her lovely upturned face in his hands and spoke the words he wanted to say on the night he moved in with her. "You're beautiful to me now and you always will be," he said. He kissed her, deeply, lovingly, longingly. He anticipated undressing her, touching and caressing her until she was ready, oh so ready, to join with him.

"Hold that thought," she said. He was not surprised. She had always been able to read his mind. He watched her drive away and waved at the flashing tail lights. Back on the street, he passed on a cab and opted instead for a nostalgic subway commute home, as he had after their intense romance rerouted his life from the Upper West Side to Brooklyn.

David met Darien on the building's second floor landing. He ran through maintenance checklists during their two flight climb to the top floor apartment and assured Darien that their home would be in good hands with him. "Go. Enjoy. No worries," David said. "All I ask is a postcard from every port of call."

Darien laughed. "That's not much payback."

"Ali's kept a roof over my head and money in my pocket for almost 30 years. It's the least I can do. Besides, Jayson and I are looking forward to touring the world vicariously. Save the details for when you come back."

The cellphone in Darien's pocket buzzed to life. Ali's cell number lit up the display. "She's probably on her way home," he said, and pressed the phone to his ear. The unfamiliar caller spoke before he could answer.

The approaching pitch of a wailing siren choked to a pitiful whine on Water Street. Strobes rotated red from the roof of the marked car that skidded to an abrupt stop at the curb in front of the building. Two men in uniform emerged from the doors marked to serve and protect. Their shoes pounded the pavement. Kenny Wong looked up from his laptop through the street level office windows. He saw them knock and pull on the door leading to the building's apartments and, when they could not gain entry, turn and backtrack to and through the main floor doors.

"This can't be good," Kenny muttered. He pushed away from his desk and rushed to meet the officers towering over a startled Mimi Teague.

"Can we help you?" he asked.

The shorter man spoke in a sharp tone through pursed lips. "We need to speak with Mr. Darien McKenna."

Mimi's hand shook as she punched her desk phone speed dial key to connect with the top floor apartment. "I'll see if he's in." Darien pushed through the office door before the first long tone sounded through her headset with David at his heels. Fear etched jagged lines across their pale faces.

The taller officer stepped forward. "Darien McKenna?"

"Yes." He spoke with control he did not feel.

"Your wife has been involved in a two-vehicle accident near West Islip on Long Island. We're here to escort you to Good Samaritan Hospital."

 "Mimi, will you call Jack?" Darien asked over his shoulder and fell in quick step behind the officer.

"I'm going with you." David followed and climbed in the cruiser's back seat next to Darien.

Jack walked off lunch down Broadway and into lower midtown past the neon flash of Times Square. Although he loved the quiet life in the New Jersey suburb where he and Beth had settled to raise a family, he was in no hurry to leave the great city. His sweet tooth stirred at the temptation of City Bakery's confectionary possibilities. He considered hiking to Union Square and catching the train to Hoboken when the cellphone in his pants pocket buzzed against his leg.

"Jack?" He couldn't identify the caller at first. But the fear in her voice came through loud and clear.

"Mimi? What's up?"

"Darien and David just left with the police. They're on their way to Good Samaritan on Long Island." A sob caught in her throat. "Something bad has happened to Ali."

The careening ride at top speed from Brooklyn to West Islip flew past in a blur of stilted and surreal slow motion images illuminated under flashing lights. The piercing scream of the siren rattled Darien's frayed nerves and escalated worry to panic. He thought he heard David pleading with Jayson to meet them at the hospital. His own soundless lips bargained with the God he had not petitioned in years.

Jayson slipped his sketchbook of fashion creations into his leather portfolio, packed up a pile of fabric swatches and headed out the front door of his Long Island client's mini-castle. "I should be ready for the first fitting by the end of next week." He walked the winding driveway to the sedan he'd rented, opened the driver's side door, and tossed the portfolio in the back seat.

The cellphone in his jacket pocket jangled. "Hello?" He nearly hung up on the sounds of heavy breathing and a high-pitched screech.

"Jayson, where are you?" Panic tumbled through the cellphone signal.

"David? I'm on Long Island. Where are you?"

"I'm in a squad car with Darien somewhere near West Islip. We're on our way to Good Samaritan Hospital." David's voice shook. "Ali's been in an accident!"

Jayson closed the car door, slipped the key in the ignition, fastened his seat belt and backed out of the driveway. "I'm only a mile or so away. I'll meet you there." He tossed the cellphone on the passenger's seat and stepped on the accelerator.

The officers accompanied Darien and David through the sliding emergency room doors and up to the glass windows that separated waiting room from medical teams. Badges and uniforms gained them immediate entry.

"I'll tell Dr. Matsen you're here." The intern's sad face and low tone dissolved Darien's last fragile shred of hope.

"Mr. McKenna?" The thin middle-aged man in scrubs and a white lab coat approached. He stood as tall as he could under the weight of slumped shoulders and the painful truth he had to deliver. "Your wife suffered traumatic internal injuries. We did everything possible. I'm so very sorry. She could not be revived."

No! No! NO!" Denial exploded in Darien's head and the shrapnel ricocheted through his body. Rage clenched his teeth and fists and sucked the breath from his lungs. Reflex locked his knees. The rest of him trembled. Behind him, David crumpled to the floor, his head in his hands. Raw anguish gushed in guttural moans from his throat. Jayson

46

knelt and held his wounded partner in the blurred periphery of Darien's tunnel vision. He forced himself to breathe. "I want to see her," he said.

"Of course," the doctor replied. He turned, waited for Darien and walked him toward a ring of closed curtain at the far end of the ER.

Jack flagged down the first available cab. "There's an extra hundred bucks in it if you get me to Long Island in a half hour or less," he'd said. The driver nodded and parted traffic out of the city, across the East River and north through Queens. Jack called Beth and left a message. The tires on the cab screeched across the asphalt leading up to the hospital entrance. Jack checked his watch, swiped his credit card and punched in the tip he'd promised. He ran past admissions to the ER.

"I'm Jack McKenna. My sister in-law was brought here."

The older woman behind the window tapped data into her computer. Jack knew when she looked up again the news was not good. "Just a moment, sir. I'll get the attending physician."

Seconds seemed like hours. Jack hit the ER doors when he heard the buzz for entry. Dr. Matsen stood on the other side. "Are you Darien's brother?" he asked.

"Yeah, I'm Jack. Where is Darien? How is Ali? Is she OK?"

The doctor pointed to a pair of metal legged chairs with yellow plastic seats and backs. Jack shook his head. A police officer approached and handed the doctor papers pinned to a clipboard. "The driver's blood alcohol level was three times the legal limit. He must have been driving like a bat out of hell." Dr. Matsen scanned the top page of the toxicology report on the clipboard and rubbed his eyes.

Jack resisted the urge to slap the clipboard out of the doctor's hand. "Will somebody please tell me what the hell is going on?"

"Walk with me," the doctor said.

Jack stepped around the thin curtain and kept his eyes on the floor. He drew in a soundless breath to center himself and prepare for what he didn't want to see.

Ali lay on the gurney covered with a white sheet. Bags of liquid suspended on I.V. poles had been pushed back. The monitors around her were silent. Darien stood beside her. He held her left hand in his. The fingers of his right hand traced the fine features of her face, carefully following each line and curve like a sighted man preparing to go blind. He gently brushed back salt-and-pepper bangs and kissed her forehead. "Ah, dear Juliet," he murmured, "why art thou yet so fair?"

Jack knew the words his brother spoke to his lost love from the countless times he'd recited and repeated them with first year English students.

Darien kissed Ali's closed eyelids.

Jack bit his lip and tasted tears.

Beth spared Darien the details of funeral arrangements.
He shook his head when his sister-in-law asked what
Ali would have wanted. She'd never made her wishes
known to him and the unthinkable had never crossed his
mind. He recoiled as though shot through the heart at
the options cremation and burial. The crypt compromise
would lay Ali to rest in the serenity of Brooklyn's Green-
Wood mausoleum surrounded by lush greenery, ponds and
well-tended pathways. Embossed lilacs, Ali's signature
fragrance and flower, would frame her inscribed name.

Faces of mourners paying respects surfaced in Darien's sea
of pain. Every "I'm so sorry" and "She's in a better place"
intensified the internal rip tide that shredded him. Jayson
stayed close to David, his oddly stoic and silent partner.
Mimi sobbed on her mother's broad stooped shoulder and
held on to her son standing tall and somber in his black suit.
Kenny's large extended family comforted and surrounded
him in mutual sorrow.

Claire Thompson, Ali's longtime publicist colleague and
friend, touched Darien's suit coat sleeve. Tears filled her
bloodshot blue eyes. "She had class in a business that
doesn't have any," she told him. "She was the best."

Chez Nous' new owner Eric and his very pregnant wife Andrea hugged him. "Sorry just doesn't cut it," he said. "This sucks big time."

"Forgive the cliché, but if there's anything we can do," Andrea began.

"Anything at all," Eric repeated.

"Thanks," was all Darien could manage.

Dan propped up Patrice through the services and steered her to Darien. She swiped tissue across cheeks streaked by tear-soaked makeup and kissed his cheek. "Thank you for her happily ever after," she whispered in his ear.

"How are you holding up, son?" Darien was gratefully aware of his father's constant presence throughout the nightmarish maelstrom. Stewart's strength had kept him from falling apart.

"I'm still standing," he answered.

After the service at the mausoleum, the McKenna family gathered at the brownstone in Hoboken where Stewart and Donna had raised their two sons. Beth arranged for a catered meal that Darien couldn't eat. He stared at the plate of food, wondered who had prepared it and why he couldn't cry.

"Anyone want more roast beef?" Beth set the replenished platter of meat in the center of the lace tablecloth dressing the dining room table.

"I'll take some more." Nathan held up his empty plate with one hand and reached for a dinner roll with the other.

"Nothing comes between a teenager and his appetite," Jack remarked.

Nathan's sister Hannah wrinkled her nose in disgust. "He's just a pig."

"He's a growing boy." Donna McKenna defended her grandson. "His Dad and Darien nearly ate us out of house and home when they were his age."

"I'm so glad we had daughters." Phyllis Doherty patted her lips with a napkin. "I know Phil wanted a son. But my delicate body just couldn't take the strain of a third pregnancy. I'd probably given birth to another daughter anyway."

"Oh, mother, please," Beth hissed under her breath. Jack poked her with his elbow and filled his fork with mashed potatoes.

Stewart passed the serving bowl of green beans to his grandson. "So, Hannah, when does fall term start at NYU?"

"The week after next. That gives me time to go with Evan to Cambridge."

"How is your young man doing at MIT?" Phyllis' eyes lit up.

"Very well. He likes it a lot."

Phil Doherty perked up. "You know what they say about MIT."

Phyllis rolled her eyes at her husband. "No. What do they say, Phil."

"M-I-T. P-h-D. M-O- N-E-Y."

"Well, I don't know if he's going for a PhD," Hannah responded. "But he is in an accelerated master's program."

"What field of study?" Phil inquired.

"Mechanical engineering and mathematics."

"Did you ever decide on a major, Hannah dear?" Phyllis asked.

"I'm going to declare math this term."

Nathan snorted between bites. "Couple of nerds."

"And you're a pig!" Hannah chastised him.

"Changing the subject entirely," Stewart interrupted. "Thank you, Beth, for making the best of a very difficult time and tragic circumstance."

"The service was lovely, dear," Donna agreed.

"Green-Wood is a prime location," Phil commented.

"Oh for God's sake, Phil!" Phyllis barked. "We're not talking about one of your real estate listings." She reached across the table and patted Darien's hand. "We're all so sorry for your loss. Take comfort in knowing she is in a better place."

She retracted her hand under Darien's withering steel grey stare. "How could she be in a better place than with me?" He took the napkin from his lap and pushed away from his untouched dinner. "Excuse me." He stood and strode to and through the kitchen. The click of the back door closing echoed through the silence.

Stewart nodded to Jack. "Excuse us." The men pushed back from the table to be with their son and brother.

Beth glared at her parents. "Congratulations, Mother and Dad. You have rewritten the definitions of rude and insensitive."

Phyllis gasped. "Well, I never!"

"No, you don't! There is no filter between what you're thinking and what you open your mouth to say for all the world to hear!"

Phyllis crossed her arms over her chest and thrust her lower lip forward in a pretend pout. "I was only trying to apologize for your father and offer our condolences."

"Don't you get it?" Beth stood bolt upright. Her chair didn't. Its wooden back hit the hardwood floor with a loud crack. "There is nothing you can say or a damn thing any of us can do! So for once in your life why couldn't you keep your selfish bullshit to yourself!"

Donna's hand flew to her mouth in a vain attempt to catch an escaping sob. Hannah wrapped a protective arm around her grandmother's shaking shoulders. Nathan stopped eating.

Phyllis dabbed at her eyes with her napkin. "How dare you speak to me that way!"

Beth turned her back on her mother's tears. Donna sputtered through hers. "It's about time somebody did."

Five pair of wide eyes fixed on Darien's distraught mother. Phil cleared his throat. "I think we'd better go," he said.

Darien stood on the back porch of his boyhood home, his arms at his side, his fists clenched and insides in knots. The chill at his core kept him from sweating in the humid late August heat. One word screamed in his head and repeated like a crazed claxon with no reset button.

Why? Why? WHY?!

The back door closed behind him. His father and brother bracketed him.

Darien spoke softly to himself yet loud enough for them to hear. "I keep waiting for this nightmare to end. I'll wake up in that hotel room in Paris where we are supposed to be right now, with Ali in my arms. She'll laugh when I tell her I dreamed she had died. Then we'll have coffee and croissants and go to The Louvre." He closed his eyes and saw her on a bench in a gallery studying a Monet. "I've never hurt this bad in all my life."

The McKenna men stood shoulder-to-shoulder, silhouetted against the setting sun.

Chapter 6

The familiar rhythm of fall term routine eased Jack away from the shock and sadness of senseless loss. Daily demands of students in classrooms and players on the field consumed his time and energy. Concern for Darien flared every time his brother refused an invitation to dinner or passed on the traditional Sunday afternoon tea and homemade cookies at their parents' home in Hoboken. Jack missed their weekly lunch at the Midtown pub. But he'd already removed that reminder from his calendar. His brother would and should have been absent for a much different reason.

Jack checked his in box before fourth period English Lit. His pulse rate rose when he saw the urgent please call message from David.

"David? It's Jack. Is Darien OK?"

"I'm not sure. Have you talked to him or seen him recently?"

Jack was ashamed to admit he had not. "I've tried calling him. So have Mom and Dad. He says he doesn't feel like dinner, a visit, or whatever fill-in-the-blank suggestion. Lately, he hasn't even been answering his phone."

"I don't think he's left the apartment since the funeral. I've been taking up a home-cooked meal once or twice a week and getting him groceries. Kenny has been covering the tab at the market. Darien doesn't invite me in. I got a quick peek at the apartment before he closed the door in my face this morning. The place is a wreck and I'm sorry to say so is he. I've never seen Darien unshaven and in serious need of a haircut. I don't think he's changed his clothes in awhile, either."

Jack sighed and slumped in a chair used by hallway monitors on the lookout for students without a valid pass. "How should I handle this?"

"Show up unannounced at the apartment. Maybe he'll let you in. And, Jack, do it soon. I'm really worried about him."

"I'll get my assistant coach to cover after-school practice. If the trains are on time, I can be there around five."

"Call when you get here. I'll come down and let you in."

Jack hesitated on the landing at the front door of the Brooklyn building's top floor apartment. Memories washed over him of the cookouts on the rooftop oasis Ali had installed to surprise Darien on his 35th birthday. And how happy his brother had been welcoming Jack and Beth through this door two days after he'd moved from his solitary life in a one room Upper West Side flat. He couldn't imagine how hard it must be for Darien to live here alone, lost in the past, his future shattered.

He knocked on the door. "Darien. It's Jack." No answer. He knocked again. "C'mon, D. I dragged my butt to Brooklyn so you know I won't go away. You might as well open the door." The sound of bare feet slapping hardwood floor preceded the click of a dead bolt lock. Jack hardly recognized the man on the other side of the open door.

Darien's black hair fell in jagged tufts along his cheekbones. A stubbly growth of equally black beard covered his cheeks, upper lip, chin and jaw. The once-white tee shirt he wore was stained and nearly every inch of his khaki cargo pants were wrinkled. Dark half-circles rimmed his eyes and their usual steel grey color had paled along with the skin Jack could see. "You look like shit," he said to his brother.

"Good to see you, too."

"Are you going to let me in?"

Darien stepped away and closed the door behind Jack. He nudged a pile of newspapers with his toes and dropped more on the pile from a stack on the sofa. "Have a seat. Want a beer?"

Jack sat down and glanced around at the debris that littered the usually uncluttered, spotless apartment. "Sure, if you can find the fridge."

Darien returned with two open bottles and pushed back an empty takeaway carton from the edge of the side table. "Sorry about the mess. I wasn't expecting company."

Jack set his bottle of beer on the only coaster he could find and rubbed his fingers across his forehead. "I don't know what to say to you, man. I won't insult you and say I know how you feel because I don't. I can't."

"You're right about that," Darien muttered.

"We all loved Ali. And we all want to help you get through this."

Darien drank his beer and rolled the empty bottle around in his hands. "When you leave here, you'll go home to Beth. It took me awhile to wrap my head around the fact that Ali won't ever come home to me again."

"She'd be so pissed off at you." Jack stood up and gestured around the room. "Look at this place, D! Then go look at yourself in the mirror. Would she recognize the man she married or the home she worked so hard to fix up and polish into the gem she was so proud to own?"

Jack crossed the room to the kitchen and began opening cupboards.

"What are you looking for?" Darien asked him.

"Garbage bags. We're going to clean this place up and take out the trash. Then you're going to shave and shower and put on some clean clothes if you've got any and we're going out to get something to eat."

Darien woke early the next morning with Jack's rebuke the night before echoing through his throbbing head. He tossed off twisted sheets and walked through rooms that didn't resemble or feel like home anymore. He stared at his reflection in the bathroom mirror and didn't know the man looking back. His eyes, the windows to his soul, were empty.

He showered, dressed, phoned a maid service to clean the apartment and speed-dialed to schedule the first available appointment for a haircut He sifted through the pile of mail that remained after he and Jack had cleared out the junk and found a window envelope with an insurance company return address. The settlement check for Ali's demolished car was inside.

He tucked the check in his wallet and cashed it on his way to the stylist. The cab ride after the haircut ended at the luxury car dealership where his wife had purchased her new and last Mercedes sedan four months before. Darien drove off the lot in a racing car green Range Rover sport SUV with a butter-colored leather interior, loaded with all the bells and whistles.

He packed the SUV with the last of what he thought he might need on a trip with no destination in mind and knocked at David's apartment door on his way out.

"I'll be gone for awhile. I have no idea how long," Darien told him.

"Where are you headed?" David asked.

"West."

Harmony

Chapter 7

Darien parked in front of his parents' home in Hoboken with the SUV's hood pointed toward the New Jersey turnpike. His mother insisted on reheating leftover pot roast, potatoes and carrots and packed him a sack of homemade cookies for the road. Stewart admired the Range Rover from the covered protection of the brownstone's front porch and hugged his son to his broad chest. Donna clung to Darien as long as she could and asked him to please call to let them know he was OK. He promised he'd keep in touch, kissed her cheek, and drove away in a mist of twilight showers.

Stewart held his weeping wife. "He's got to work through this in his own way," he told her and said a silent prayer that he would.

The turnpike turned to interstate at Teaneck. Sometime after midnight, somewhere in the Commonwealth of Pennsylvania, Darien pulled off the endless ribbon of asphalt and into the first motel parking lot with a lit vacancy sign. He dozed fully-clothed on a double bed covered by a threadbare chenille spread until the sun in his eyes through paper-thin curtains signaled the time to move on. After a quick shower, shave, and change of clothes, he turned in the room key, drove up to and through the nearest fast food pick-up window, and resumed the unplanned course toward a future he could not foresee and a life he hadn't planned.

The monotonous montage of mile markers and exit signs came to road-weary end at a motel in Ohio. Loneliness slipped into the empty passenger seat and buckled up for the long haul somewhere in Indiana. Darien ordered the lunch special of the day at a roadside restaurant on the outskirts of a dot on the map in downstate Illinois. He fed half of a tasteless takeaway sandwich he knew he'd never eat to a stray dog roaming the diner parking lot. The friendly Beagle-mix jumped into the SUV when Darien opened the driver's side door.

"Hey, buddy. You need a ride home?" Darien scanned the tags that dangled from the dog's cracked leather collar. "Oslo" had been vaccinated against rabies. Darien went back in the diner and asked the cashier if she knew who owned Oslo. Her watery blue eyes set close together in a round middle-aged face squinted and glanced past Darien to the grinning dog framed in the SUV's windshield. "That dog belongs to the Fishers. He digs his way out of their bag yard about once a week." She scribbled notes on the back of a useless receipt. "Take him to the pound. Lilah will fetch him when she gets off work."

Darien followed her directions to the animal shelter on a gravel road beyond the last sign at the edge of town. Oslo barked at a Husky secured behind a cement floored kennel run severed from nature by a wrap around tower of chain link fence. The dirty white dog tugged on a frayed rope held at the opposite end by a thin man with a receding hairline wearing baggy and faded hospital green scrubs.

The attendant at the front desk knew the Beagle-mix. She thanked Darien for retrieving Oslo and assured him the dog would be home before the shelter closed at five. Darien stuffed a $50 bill in the donation box on the counter and walked back to his car. The Husky behind the fence leaped into the air and caught the rope tossed by the thin man.

"That's a beautiful dog." Darien squatted and curled his fingers around the chain link. The Husky let go of the frayed toy and trotted to the fence. She sniffed Darien's fingers. Her pointed ears swiveled forward. Her intense blue eyes stared into his.

"Yeah, she is." The shelter worker walked up and stood behind the thick fox-like tail wagging side to side like a waving flag on a pole. "It's a shame she didn't pass."

"What do you mean by didn't pass?" Darien asked without looking up or away from the Husky.

"Shelter manager says she's a bite risk. I don't think so and I've been taking care of her in strays for two weeks now. But," he shrugged his shoulders, "that's not my call."

Darien stood. "So what happens to her now?"

The kennel worker looked up at him. "They'll put her down. Probably tomorrow."

"No, they won't." Darien turned and walked back through the shelter's door. "Excuse me." The attendant behind the desk stopped writing and pushed aside a pile of paper charts.

"Can I help you?" she asked.

"I'd like to adopt the white dog in the run outside."

The attendant sifted through the pile of charts. "Which dog is that?"

"The female Husky with blue eyes. The guy out there with her said she didn't pass."

"You'll need to talk to the shelter manager." The attendant reached for the phone. After a quick one-sided conversation, an overweight woman oozing attitude marched through a door marked 'Employees only.' The pea green scrubs she wore stretched over inflated rolls of belly fat below a bra that strained to hold her puffed up breasts. Her ramrod military demeanor raised Darien's defenses. He braced to fight for the white dog's life.

"Can I help you," she said with no hint of question in her tone of voice.

"I've already been asked and answered," he replied. "I'd like to adopt the white Husky."

She crossed her arms between belly and breasts. "That dog is not available for adoption."

"May I ask why not?"

"She did not pass the behavior assessment."

"Do you have guidelines and standards for assessing behavior?"

"Of course we do."

"May I see them, please?"

Her cheeks flushed on either side of pursed pale lips. "Animal behavior is assessed subjectively."

"You mean arbitrarily."

"Is there a problem?" A younger woman with big hair and wide hips appeared behind the flustered shelter manager. Darien sensed an easy target ready and willing to give in to his good looks and charm. He smiled at her. She smiled back.

"There's no problem," he said. "I'm sorry. We have not been properly introduced. I'm Darien McKenna."

"He picked up the Fishers' dog at the diner and brought him in," the attendant explained.

"That was very kind of you." The younger woman extended her hand. "I'm Donna Fisher, the shelter director."

Darien took the hand she offered in both of his. "My mother's name is Donna."

The director dropped her chin to her chest and looked away. The dimples in her cheeks deepened. The unaffected shelter manager bristled between them. "He wants to adopt the white Husky we tested this morning."

"I saw the dog in the run outside when I drove in," Darien explained.

"I'm sorry, but that dog is not available for adoption," the director responded.

"That's what I told him!" the shelter manager snarled.

"Could I at least meet the dog?" Darien asked.

The director hesitated. "That dog tried to bite me. You must understand the shelter cannot be held responsible for any injury to you."

Darien nodded. "I'll take my chances."

She nodded to the shelter manager. "Have Craig bring the dog to the meet and greet room." The shelter manager glared at Darien but snapped to and followed orders.

Darien sat in a metal folding chair and waited in a cramped room that needed a fresh coat of paint. The kennel worker from the outdoor run appeared in the doorway with the white dog on a leash. "Good luck," he said and closed the door behind the dog's bushy tail.

"Hello, girl," Darien said in a low voice. The dog stared at him. Neither of them moved. "I need a traveling companion. I don't know where I'm going or how long we'll be on the road. But I'd like you to come along with me." The dog's ears perked up and swiveled forward.

"Would that be OK with you?"

The dog inched toward him, powerful muscles built to pull a sled gliding beneath thick layers of fur protection against the harsh Siberian climate. She raised a webbed front paw to his knee and nudged his hand with her cold, wet nose. He rubbed her ears and shook the paw she'd offered. "Done deal." He picked up his end of the leash and led her to the front counter. "I'll take her. Let's make this happen," he said. He signed the required paperwork, paid the adoption fee, and led the dog to take her place in the passenger's seat beside him.

Darien's search for dog friendly lodgings that night scored a multiple night stay in luxury accommodations at a boutique hotel in Davenport, Iowa. The concierge recommended a veterinarian to administer the required rabies vaccine. Darien purchased top quality food and all the necessary supplies for his companion's comfort and safety while the pet store groomer washed away shelter soil and smell. He curled up in the king-sized bed against the first warmth he'd felt beside him since Ali and realized the Husky didn't have a name.

"Who are you?" he asked her. She rested her chin on his chest, sighed through her nose and smacked her lips in a canine show of contentment. He ruffled her clean and perfumed fur through his fingers. "Even after a bath, you're not quite white, are you, girl? You're the color of my mom's lace tablecloth." He snuggled under the royal plum satin covered down comforter, yawned and closed his eyes. "Good night, Ivory."

A late October rainstorm and detours into and around Iowa City snarled traffic to an agonizing crawl. Frustrated and bored with interstate travel, Darien took the next exit and pointed the Range Rover north on the less travelled Highway 1. Five miles off the beaten path, heavy clouds unleashed relentless curtains of rain. Darien pulled over and slammed on the brakes to avoid striking flares behind a disabled car parked up ahead. Tail lights on the white pickup truck flashed on either side of the Easter egg purple truck topper.

The flash flood from the sky ended as abruptly as it began. "Stay here, girl," he told the white dog. Darien grabbed a flashlight from the glove compartment and walked the shoulder of the road toward the truck. He tapped on the foggy driver's side window.

"Hey! Do you need any help?"

The window opened a crack, then an inch and bit more. Emerald green eyes peered out over the glass. "No, thank you," the woman inside replied in a smoky voice. "There's a tow truck on the way." The window closed before Darien could say another word.

He returned to his car in a steady drip of cold rain. He closed the door on the dampness, buckled up, turned the key in the ignition and settled into the warmth of the heated seat.

Ivory licked the rain from his cheek. He rubbed her ears. "Geez, Ivory, is my road funk that bad?" He checked for oncoming traffic and drove away from the flares and blinking hazard lights.

The weather refused to break. After the third downpour in less than 30 miles on the road to nowhere, Darien sought refuge in a town with a name that rhymed with his. The first motel on the right hand side of the highway leading to Marion accepted pets and offered a bonus guest laundry service to clean his suitcase full of dirty clothes. Darien downed three cups of complimentary hot coffee, ordered pizza delivered to his room, and made a mental note to use the motel's fitness and weight room in the morning.

"Darien McKenna?"

Darien ceased his pounding assault on the fitness room treadmill and wiped sweat from his eyes with a towel. He didn't recognize the muscular man with the buzz cut on the other side of the backlit display or the navy blue anchor tattoo on his forearm.

"Brian Casey." The man stuck out his hand. "Urban planning architect out of Chicago. We worked together on the World Trade Center project."

"Right." Darien wiped his hand with the towel and matched Brian's strong handshake with his own.

"What the hell are you doing in Iowa?" Brian suddenly dropped his tone and smile. "Sorry to hear about your wife."

Darien stepped off the treadmill and quickly changed the subject. "I've got time on my hands and a lot of states I haven't seen."

"Long road trip?"

"Something like that."

"Just passing through or looking for something to do?"

"Pretty much the former."

Brian's smile returned. "Maybe I can talk you into the latter. I'm doing a favor for an old friend who's put his life savings on the line opening two restaurants by New Year's Eve, one in Cedar Rapids just north of here the other up river in Dubuque. Both of them will be upscale by Iowa standards. I could sure use your help. Are you up for a challenge?"

Darien rubbed the back of his neck with the damp towel. "I could be."

Brian's easy smile got bigger. "Good. You got plans for breakfast?"

"I haven't got plans for much of anything."

"I'll meet you in the lobby in a half hour. We'll head down the road and talk details over a plate of Iowa pork and eggs. My treat."

Darien reserved a suite at the motel through the end of the year. He hung and folded what he needed into the suite's armoire and drawers and stacked the rest of what he'd brought with him from Brooklyn in short term storage. The motel staff reported no problems with Ivory in his absence. The dog lounged away the hours on quilted fleece bedding behind the open door of the crate he'd bought for her security and comfort and patiently waited for her master's return.

Darien ate a light breakfast before driving to Dubuque for an early morning consultation with the restaurant's newly-hired chef. Hunger drove him off Highway 13 in search of a mid-day meal on the way back to Marion. The two-lane exit road into Harmony curved around a football practice field and the adjacent high school Home of the Fighting Hens. Signs to "Hank's Longhorn Café – Best Eats this Side of Cedar Rapids" pointed toward the town's six-block central business district.

Darien parked next to an older model white pickup truck equipped with a purple topper over the flatbed. He opened the door to a crowded dining room and the pungent boiled cabbage assault to his keen sense of smell.

Patrons of all shapes and sizes filled every hard surface booth and mismatched wooden chair around four top tables. Darien spotted a lone empty stool at the U-shaped counter centered at the core of the diner. He routed through the maze of tables and stood at the stool next to an attractive young woman with a sketch pad and pencil. Her thick mane of copper-colored hair formed a soft chignon at the nape of her long neck. The black leather jacket she wore rode just above the waistline of snug fit jeans hugging long slender legs. Her ankle boots reminded Darien of the required fashion statement worn by women back home in Manhattan. *But they'd never wear a plaid shirt,* he thought.

"Is this seat taken?"

Emerald green eyes he remembered from a half-open driver's side window in the rain focused on him. She handed him a menu. "It is now."

He took the menu and straddled the stool. "What do you recommend?"

"Anything but the special of the day. Unless you like cabbage stew."

"Not so much. Thanks for the warning."

A sweating glass of ice water appeared on the counter in front of Darien. "What's your pleasure, handsome?" Twinkling brown eyes set in the smiling face of the waitress reminded him of Ali. He swallowed the gathering lump in his throat. "Just a cup of coffee for now."

"You got it." A white china cup filled with black coffee and a small silver pitcher of cream on the side materialized within minutes. "Here's your soup, honey." The waitress set a bowl of clear broth packed with chicken and noodles in front of the young woman.

"I see your truck is on the road again."

Her hand holding the spoon stopped in mid stir. The dazzling green eyes narrowed then opened wide. "You're the guy who almost took out my flares."

"It was raining pretty hard."

"True enough." Her breath scattered steam rising from the broth on her spoon. "Sorry I was so rude. I was having a bad day."

"I've had a few of those myself lately." He stopped the waitress on her next pass past. "I'll have the reuben and home fries, please." He ignored the cream, raised the coffee cup, smiled and nodded at her. "Let's start over. I'm Darien."

She smiled and nodded. "I'm Miranda."

He pointed at the sketch pad. "Habit or hobby?"

"Neither. I'm an artist."

"Really? What medium?"

"I'll do whatever the client wants, but watercolor is my preference and my passion."

"Why watercolor? I'm no artist, but I would think acrylic paints or even oils are easier to work with."

"That's exactly why I prefer watercolor. It's rather like taming an animal. The wash is wild and free. I apply the colors and control the brush strokes. But the element of danger is always there. One slip and ..." she tore a page from her sketch book and crumpled it in her hands. "Start over."

"Sort of like experimenting with ingredients for a new entrée on the dinner menu," he said. "Sometimes it works and when it doesn't the line cooks get fed."

She grinned at him. "I'm guessing that you are a chef."

He shrugged. "I used to be."

"What are you now?"

"A traveler."

"Are you traveling alone?"

"I have a dog."

"Is your dog in the car?"

"No, she's back at the motel in Marion."

Miranda finished her soup and unzipped the small black leather purse at the end of the strap over her shoulder. "Well, if she needs to see a vet before you hit the road again, the best in the county is right across the street." She dropped dollar bills and coins on the counter and called out to the waitress. "Hey, Shayla. Can you pack up a couple orders of the dinner special for Sam and me later on?"

"I always do, honey," Shayla replied.

Miranda slid off the stool. "Safe travels, Darien." He watched her thread her way through the thinning lunch crowd and open the door on a grey November day. He paid his tab and left a generous tip, believing the artist with dazzling green eyes would take home dinners that night for herself and a significant other named Sam.

Chapter 8

Ivory's hacking cough and persistent head shake woke Darien at daybreak. "What's wrong, girl?" he asked the distressed dog. He filled her water bowl but she wouldn't drink. His concern rose when she turned down her favorite bacon-flavored treat. He tapped his laptop to life and went online to find the phone number of the only veterinarian in Harmony, left a voice mail message, showered, dressed and coaxed Ivory into the Range Rover.

He parked the car in front of the single story cement block building as the lights inside flickered on. "C'mon, girl." He led Ivory under the clinic's red and white striped canvas awning and the shingle over the door that read Samantha McCullough DVM. Sunshine yellow walls welcomed clients and pet patients into the small yet sufficient waiting room. Vacant chairs lined up like soldiers on either side of a corner table covered by stacks of magazines. A calming watercolor landscape of a serene high blue sky summer day over a lake dotted by sailboats hung on the far wall behind a bank of file cabinets and work station with the usual office equipment. The accompanying reception desk and chair on wheels behind it was empty.

"Hello?" Darien called out.

"Be right there." The voice sounded familiar to him. The tall, slender woman dressed in jeans and a denim shirt with a tidy mound of copper hair wound at the collar was unmistakably Miranda.

"You again!" she said. "And this must be your traveling companion." She extended her fisted fingers for the white dog to sniff. "What's your name, beautiful?"

"Her name is Ivory," Darien answered. "I called and left a message."

"Oh, yes. Coughing and shaking her head." She led Darien and his dog around the corner she'd appeared from to the first room on the right. A young woman in bright yellow scrubs greeted him with a wide smile.

"Hi, I'm Doc Sam." She reached out to shake Darien's hand, dropped to one knee and tossed a thick, wavy ponytail of honey blonde hair over her shoulder. "Hello, princess," she said. "I need to check you out, OK?"

Ivory dipped her head and nudged the doctor's arm in apparent consent. "What a good girl you are," she said and began the exam. "How long have you had her?" the veterinarian asked.

"A couple of weeks maybe. I got her from a shelter."

Sam sat back on her heels. "She's got kennel cough and an ear infection. That's pretty common, coming from a shelter environment. Otherwise, she's in pretty good shape." Sam patted Ivory's head and stood up. At full height in soft-soled flat shoes, the top of her head was almost level with Darien's broad shoulders. "A few days on meds and she'll be back to her old self in no time. I would like to see her again in a couple weeks."

Darien nodded. "I can bring her in on my way to Dubuque."

"What's in Dubuque, if you don't mind my asking?"

"I'm helping a colleague open a restaurant there and another in Cedar Rapids."

"Mira said you were a chef."

"I assume you are referring to Miranda, artist and apparently your receptionist."

Sam laughed and her robin's egg blue eyes twinkled. "She's all that and my sister."

"So you're Sam who got Hank's dinner special."

"One and the same. You should try the meatloaf. It's the best!"

Darien's stomach growled. "Sorry. I didn't have breakfast."

Miranda poked her head around the open exam room door. "Neither did I and Buck is known for his kick-ass western omelet."

Sam rolled her eyes and licked her lips. "I haven't had one of those in a long time."

"Your ten o'clock cancelled," Miranda told her sister and winked at Darien. "We could let him pick up the breakfast tab in exchange for the office visit."

Darien grinned. "I'll gladly pay for both. What about Ivory?"

"She can sleep off the first dose of meds in my office," Sam said to Darien, "and we can bring her back a little treat from Buck's kitchen."

"Sounds like a plan," he agreed.

Buck Malone's western omelet exceeded Darien's expectations, and he told him so. The large man with the beefy hands, brown hair and eyes and a single gold front tooth grinned an easy smile between a full beard and mustache. "Comes from years of practice feeding ranch hands in Colorado," he explained.

"He cooked me up one of those and proposed," said the waitress introduced to Darien as Shayla, Buck's wife and co-owner of the café. "I had to say yes."

"Been in business here long?" Darien asked.

Buck glanced at his wife and scratched his head. "Going on three years now, I think. Is that about right darlin'?"

Shayla nodded. "We came to Iowa when Buck took a job his cousin got him at the post office in Marion." She wrinkled her nose and the sprinkle of freckles temporarily disappeared. "But after living and working on a ranch in Durango for years, neither one of us much liked living in an apartment building. So we worked out a lease-with-option-to-buy deal with the previous owner of this place and moved in upstairs."

"So Hank was the previous owner?"

"No, sir. This is Hank." Buck reached down and scratched behind the erect ears of a shepherd-mix mutt with a curled-up tail and multi-colored patchwork fur coat. "He kept showing up at the back door begging for food. So we took him in and named the place after him. He's been the boss ever since." Buck brought his index finger to his lips and made a shushing sound. "Don't tell the health inspector."

Darien savored each bite of omelet and wheat toast. The congenial banter between friends and family briefly relieved the chronic ache of loss and loneliness. The obvious sibling affection and connection between Sam and Miranda reminded him of lunch at the pub with Jack in a distant happier past.

That night, Darien turned out the bedside lamp and called New Jersey. "Hey, Jack. Yeah, I'm still in Iowa. I miss you, too, man."

Chapter 9

Days and weeks sped by, marked by auto pilot runs on bland highways between restaurants in a dead heat towards the New Year's Eve finish line. Darien sought regular solace in the familiar clatter and hum of Hank's Longhorn Café.

Buck topped up Darien's cup of coffee for a third time on a mid-week late morning. "Mind if I ask something that's none of my business?"

Darien looked up from the latest text message displayed on his phone. "What's on your mind?"

"You've been in here just about every other day for over a month," he nodded toward the nearly full bowl of beef barley soup, "and I know you're not coming back for the food."

Darien grinned at the big middle-aged man behind the counter. "Harmony is half way between the restaurants I'm opening in Cedar Rapids and Dubuque."

The big man's eyebrows arched up. "You own two restaurants?"

"No. I'm working with the owner."

"You a chef?"

"I was years ago."

"Oh, yeah? Where 'bouts?"

"Manhattan."

Buck's eyebrows arched in surprise. "New York City?"
Darien nodded. Buck looked down at the bowl again.
"Sorry about the soup."

Darien shrugged. "Hey, you work with what you got."

Buck wiped down the counter with his ever-present bar
rag and shook his head. "It's a straight shot between Cedar
Rapids and Dubuque on Highway 151 and it's a better road
to boot. There's other places to squat and gobble, even here
in Harmony. Hell, the bar and grill down the street serves
up a pretty decent burger."

"I prefer to grill my own." Darien's eyes scanned the
restaurant's windows for movement on the street.

Buck checked his watch. "She won't be in for another half
hour or so."

"Excuse me?" Darien responded.

Buck grunted. "Be-ins it's not the food that brings you
here, I wager it's the company you're wantin' to keep."
He leaned over the counter toward Darien. "I'm not sure
which one of the McCullough sisters has caught your eye.
But if I were a betting man, my money'd be on Miranda."

Darien frowned and straightened on the stool. "What makes
you say that?"

Buck stepped back and held up his hands. "Don't get me wrong. Doc Sam is a fine looking filly. But there's not an available man in this town or the county who isn't interested in Miranda. And she's not interested in any man here." His steady gaze sized up Darien, from his high style urban attire to the face and form he'd watched women stare at and heard them giggle and buzz about in their sisterhood circles. "You're not from here, though." Buck whistled a long sigh through his teeth. "A man could lose himself in those pretty eyes and that fiery hair."

Shayla set a basket of onion rings in front of a customer seated next to Darien and poked her husband in the ribs. "Dwayne! Those B-L-Ts won't make themselves!"

"The name's Buck, woman!" He pretended to scold her, but the spark of humor dancing in his eyes gave him away. "She knows how to get me going," he muttered and headed for the kitchen.

The restaurant in Cedar Rapids was ready to open a full week ahead of schedule. Although panic simmered just below boil at the restaurant in Dubuque, the items on Darien's detailed list of tasks to opening night were down to a manageable few. He was about ready to move on, to where he wasn't sure. He left Cedar Rapids craving a fine bottle of wine and deli delicacies to feed his body and settle his mind. The road to comfort food and drink led him to downtown Iowa City and a chance meeting with Miranda at the market cash register.

Darien glanced over her shoulder into the shopping cart of items she'd selected and critiqued her choices of cheeses. "You really should try the Maytag blue," he recommended.

Startled, she jumped and tumbled backward against his chest. He caught her in his arms. Embarrassed, she sputtered an apology over her shoulder. Her eyes flew open when she recognized the man whose shoes she'd just stepped on. "Still try to come to my rescue?" she asked.

"So it would seem."

Groceries bagged, they walked together into snowflakes falling from a slate grey December sky. Miranda shivered and clutched her wool scarf under her chin. "I've lived here all my life, but winter always takes me by surprise."

Darien pointed to a red neon store front sign on the opposite side of the plaza. "Can I interest you in a cup of coffee?"

"That's a fabulous idea."

The whoosh of steam through an espresso maker and the aroma of fresh brew greeted them on the other side of the coffee shop door. They chose a window table, slung coats across the ladder backs of the chairs, and ordered tall lattes. Miranda sipped from her cup and licked froth from her lips. "I can't remember coffee ever tasting this good."

"It definitely hits the spot," he agreed.

She sighed at the shoppers rushing past the twinkling holiday displays and bundled up volunteers ringing bells over kettles. "Everyone is in such a hurry. They don't stop for a minute to enjoy the season." She tapped the vinyl tablecloth with her fingernails. "So! What are your plans for Christmas?"

Darien's blank expression surprised her almost as much as his response. "I … hadn't noticed. That is, I haven't … I don't have any plans."

"You're kidding me, right? Tomorrow is Christmas Eve."

Ali's birthday, he thought, and the mask he'd worn since her death slipped away with the blood from his face.

"Darien! What's wrong?" She reached for his hand. He pulled it away. Her hands dropped to her lap. "I'm sorry."

He shook his head and rubbed his temples. "No, I'm sorry. I guess I've been pre-occupied counting down the days until the restaurants opened."

The concern in her eyes and warmth of her smile cracked the ice around the self-constructed fortress around Darien's heart. "Look, why don't you have Christmas dinner with Sam and me? It's just the two of us since Dad passed away. But we always put up a tree and Sam cooks an awesome turkey with all the trimmings. I do the dessert," she added with a hint of pride.

"Thanks for the invitation but I couldn't …"

"I'm sure Sam would appreciate some help in the kitchen. And Ivory could play with Dave in the back yard."

"Dave?"

"Sam's Malamute. He's huge and harmless, just a big old love bug."

"Well, I don't …"

"I'll call Sam right now."

"Miranda, wait, I'm not …"

"Hey, little sister," she said into the cellphone. "Darien and Ivory are coming to our house for Christmas. Get out the good china and tell Dave to behave."

Darien muttered apologies and excuses for skipping Christmas dinner in Harmony right up to the moment he stood alongside Ivory on the front porch of the McCullough family home. He'd considered calling to cancel even as he bought a bottle of the best merlot he could find in Iowa City and picked up a dozen red and white roses.

The Craftsman-style wood front door opened before he could knock.

"Merry Christmas!" A red-faced Sam, wearing jeans and a white sweater protected by an apple green bib apron stepped back to admit Darien and his dog. Ivory sniffed the air and followed her nose around the corner to the kitchen partially hidden from view behind saloon-like swinging half doors. Darien handed Sam the wine and roses. "Oh, Darien, they're lovely!" She read the label on the wine bottle. "Sorry, I don't know much about wine. Should I put this in the fridge?"

He shook his head. "Red wine is served at room temperature."

"Mira," Sam called to her sister. "Can you grab a vase and put some water in it, please?"

"I will as soon as I get the pie out of the oven."

"Let me take your coat." Sam hung Darien's black cashmere top coat on the wood coat and hat tree near the front door. She stepped through the high overhead archway that defined the modest one room living space and set the wine and flowers on the dining table set for three. Rectangular wool area rugs dyed in shades of royal blue and burgundy protected polished oak hardwood floors. An overstuffed sofa and a pair of mission-style rocking chairs and end tables framed the cozy front room area around a wood burning fireplace. Needles and tinsel fallen from the heavily decorated six-foot Scotch pine Christmas tree in the front porch picture window littered the lids of presents stripped of holiday wrap and ribbon.

"Why do you need a vase?" Miranda pushed through the swinging doors carrying a cut crystal vase half-filled with water. She wore an apron identical to her sister's over black jeans and a cowl-necked sweater tinted the color of her eyes. Her copper-colored hair tied back with an emerald green ribbon streamed thick and long past her elbows.

"For the roses Darien brought," Sam answered and gestured toward the table.

Miranda removed florist's paper from the stems of the fragile blooms. "They're beautiful."

So are you. The thought, and rush of visceral emotion with it, surprised Darien. "Can I help with dinner?" he asked.

"I was hoping you would," Sam said and led the way to the eclectic kitchen of original wood cabinets, modern appliances and a retro yellow and white linoleum tile floor.

Time both stood still and sailed past in an afternoon Darien had both dreaded and needed. Ivory hid behind Darien when Dave lumbered in from outside. After a few furtive sniffs, touched noses and play bows with tails in the air, the dogs trotted outside to explore and chase each other around the fenced in quarter acre of snow-covered ground. Sam called the dogs in after dinner to feast on a mix of veterinarian-approved table scraps and kibble. The three friends settled around the fireplace with the last of the wine poured into glasses. Dave flopped down and snored in front of the glowing hearth. Ivory slept with her chin on Darien's foot.

Sam and Miranda shared the highs, lows and losses of the close-knit McCullough family. Their mother had worked as a manicurist and cut hair at a local salon until she passed away from breast cancer when Sam was four years old. Eight-year-old Miranda took over most of the household chores and supervised her sister during the long hours their father worked as a mechanic at the shop he owned in town. Miranda learned the basics of bookkeeping managing Big Jim McCullough's accounts payable and receivable. She finished her first two years of higher education at the community college in Cedar Rapids and had enrolled at the University of Iowa to study studio art in the fall. The heart attack that took their father that summer changed everything. Miranda quit college and worked any job she could find to keep a roof over their heads until her younger sister finished high school. Sam's academic honors and experience as a young apprentice to Harmony's only veterinarian during her junior high and high school years realized her dream of acceptance into Iowa State University and the College of Veterinary Medicine. Miranda worked, paid the bills, and saved to help open and invest in Sam's practice. Sam leveraged future earnings with a loan that helped her sister open an art studio and gallery in Harmony.

"So, we've told you our story," Sam prodded Darien. "What's yours?"

He edited the details, omitting any bits related to his life with Ali. He told them about his family in New Jersey and briefly summarized his experience-driven career that led from line cook in a squat and gobble to executive chef at Chez Nous and culinary consulting.

"So opening the restaurants brought you to Iowa?" Sam asked.

"Not exactly," he answered and offered no more.

"Well, I'm ready for pie and coffee," Miranda said.

"Me, too," Sam agreed.

"Let me help you," Darien offered. Miranda's hand on his shoulder stopped him from leaving the comfort of the sofa's cushion.

"You're our guest," she said and bent down to pet the sleeping dog at his feet. "Both of you."

Sam waited until her sister was out of earshot. She leaned forward in the rocking chair and kept her voice low. "How long before you leave?"

"Next week. Why?"

"I'd like you to talk to Miranda about going back to get her degree."

Darien shook his head. "I'm hardly the best person to encourage her. My parents and brother went to college. I didn't. "

Sam sat back and sighed. "I guess you're right."

"Have you talked to her?"

"Only every day. I'm pretty sure she wants to finish what she started. I admit I feel guilty that she didn't and hasn't mostly because of me. Every time I bring up the subject, she says she'll think about it when we're out of debt. Which at this rate will be the twelfth of never."

"Sam, this is all really none of my business. But I do understand living life on your own terms. "

"You're saying I should let her."

"Exactly."

Chapter 10

Ice pellets bounced off the Range Rover's hood and windshield two hours before midnight on New Year's Eve. Darien fled a flurry of handshakes in Dubuque ahead of the predicted major winter storm. He reached the hotel without incident, walked Ivory across the least treacherous patches of pavement and packed up the last of what he wouldn't need the next morning. He called and wished his brother a Happy New Year as the televised ball dropped in Times Square and let waves of homesickness rock him to sleep.

He dreamed of his first New Year's Eve with Ali, saw the snow fall on Brooklyn Bridge beyond their kitchen window, felt the warmth of her body under silk and breathed in the lilac scent of her. He awoke aroused and alone.

After a cold shower to clear his head and dampen sexual need, Darien wrapped himself in a thick cotton towel and robe the motel provided and answered his buzzing cellphone.

"Darien? It's Miranda. Are you still in Marion?"

He was surprised at the pleasure of hearing her voice. "Yes. I'm almost ready to go."

"Not today you won't. Have you looked outside?"

"No, I haven't." He opened the heavy drapery and gauzy curtain. A frozen world awaited on the other side of the window.

"Please tell me you won't try to drive on two inches of ice under eight inches of snow," she cautioned.

He sighed. "I guess not."

"Would you call and say goodbye before you do leave?"

"I'll do better than that. How about lunch at Hank's for auld lang syne?"

She laughed. "It's a date! Happy New Year, Darien."

"Happy New Year, Miranda."

The Iowa Department of Transportation declared the state's highways passable two days later. Darien phoned Miranda as promised.

"I'm just about to lock up the office. I'll meet you across the street."

"Is Sam joining us?"

"She's out on a rural call. I don't think she'll be back for lunch."

"Then I guess I'll have to stay for dinner, too."

"Bring Ivory with you. We could take her for a long walk, maybe let her run off leash."

Darien told the front desk clerk he would be checking out the next day, low-whistled his dog into the Range Rover's passenger seat, and headed north to Harmony.

Shayla had packed lunch to go for two and a treat for Ivory on Darien's promise that he would be back for dinner. Darien piloted roads that traversed the frosted countryside Miranda knew so well. They stopped at an abandoned campground where Ivory tracked and chased small prey through the snow and returned to the welcome warmth of the car's heated seats. They ate corned beef on rye and double chocolate brownies with a windshield view of a magical winter world bathed in the blue tint of seasonal sunlight. Miranda's chattered small talk directed Darien down lane ways she and Sam had grown up exploring on bicycles in the promise of spring and the searing heat of summer.

"That's the old Meyer homestead." She pointed to an abandoned two-story farmhouse perched at the apex of a gentle hill at a T-junction a half-mile ahead. "Sam and I made up stories about the people who might have lived there. When I closed my eyes, I could see the man who built it carrying his bride across the threshold. I could hear their babies crying upstairs in the bedroom. The farmer's dog is asleep on the back porch and wakes up to follow him to the barn every day to tend the horses. The trees in the orchard are loaded with apples and the corn in the field whispers in the wind." She leaned forward and squinted into the glare. "Darien! Pull over! There's a car in the driveway!"

He maneuvered the Range Rover around the gravel road corner and turned to the left onto cracked and rutted cement. Miranda and Ivory bounded out of the vehicle before he could unlatch his seat belt.

"Hello?" Miranda called. She and the white dog beside her trotted past the parked fire engine red late model Volvo station wagon and onto the sagging front porch of the farmhouse. A middle-aged man in a black wool top coat opened the front door.

"Hello!" He greeted her with a broad smile and an outstretched hand. "Stan Hale is the name and real estate is my game." He shook her hand and patted Ivory's head. "Beautiful dog."

"Thank you." Darien climbed the porch steps behind her.

"Is this property for sale?" Miranda asked.

"It will be as soon as the appraisal is done and the ink on the paperwork is dry."

"Can we go in?"

Stan removed his black felt hat and scratched his balding head. "Well, now, the old girl is pretty rustic. She really isn't up to show quality. But if you want to take a look around, be my guest."

"Yes!" Miranda clapped her hands and skipped past Stan into the setting of her childhood fantasies.

Stan wound up for the pitch. "You and the missus in the market for a home?

Darien stammered a hurried response. "What? No. She's not, I mean, we're not ..."

Miranda bounced down the stairs from the homestead's second floor, her face flushed with excited possibility. "Oh, Darien! I can hear the babies crying!"

"You sure about that?" Stan asked and poked his elbow into Darien's ribs.

Miranda grabbed Darien's hand with both of her own and pulled him through the doorway. "Come with me," she pleaded. He followed her through room after room of crumbling plaster and peeling wallpaper, water-stained wood, cracked and broken windows. Where he saw a scope of work not worth the obvious escalating cost of repair, she saw potential for redemption, resurrection, and renewal.

"Either one of these spaces would make a fabulous studio." They stood in the upstairs hallway at the entrance to two of four bedrooms. Miranda walked diagonal lines to the corner between windows set in perpendicular walls. "The natural light is perfect. And look at the views of the fields and the orchard! I'd be inspired every season of the year."

Darien could see her sitting here, a lapboard across her thighs and knees, washing the paper on it with chosen colors from dipped brushes. He saw himself looking over her shoulder, filling his hands with her thick hair, leaning into her, kissing her neck, breathing her in, hearing her sigh. He shook his head to erase the image from his mind. "We better go," he said and turned on his heel toward the stairway and a safe exit.

Stan was waiting for them at the bottom of the stairs.

"What's the asking price?" Miranda asked the realtor.

"You can't be serious about buying this place," Darien cautioned.

"Of course not," she said. "I don't have that kind of money. I'm just curious."

Stan scratched bare skin on his head again. "Well, I just located a distant relative of the owner who got stiffed when the contract to buy went bad 10 or 12 years back. The family is eager to sell. I'm sure they'd consider any reasonable offer."

A gust of wind blew the front door open and Ivory trotted through. She shook off snow from the field she'd explored, sniffed every corner of the room and settled with a thump in front of the silent fireplace.

"Looks like someone has made herself right at home," Stan remarked. "How about it? We can write up an offer on the spot."

"I'm leaving town tomorrow," Darien started to say. But he couldn't form the words that he knew would dim the shining hope in Miranda's beautiful eyes. "This place needs a lot of work," he said instead.

"The sellers know that," Stan replied, "and that's to your advantage."

"It could be fun putting this place back together," Miranda said. "This should be a piece of cake compared to remodeling and opening restaurants."

"I oversee the design and set up kitchen operations. I've never actually swung the hammer," Darien protested.

"I have," Miranda responded. "I knocked down walls, put up drywall, put in windows, whatever I had to do to build my studio on the cheap and get Sam's office up and running. I'd love to help you bring this old house back."

What is it with you and strong-willed women, D, he asked himself, recalling David's description of Ali tossing rotted wood and debris into a Dumpster four floors below during the painstaking renovation of her Brooklyn building and their eventual home. Darien glanced from Miranda to Stan and made a low-ball cash bid that even he would refuse.

The agent shook his head. "I don't think they'll go for that. This house sits on 14 acres of prime Iowa farmland that's worth more than what you've offered. You could tear down the house and build brand new for less than it would cost to renovate."

"Oh, no!" Miranda cried out.

Darien stood firm. "That's my final offer."

"OK," said Stan. "I'll present it to the family and let you know what they say."

Miranda announced the news to the dinner crowd at Hank's. "Darien made an offer on the Meyer farm!"

The locals rolled out rounds of questions and comments between bites.

"That old place is for sale?" "How long has it been since the last Meyer moved out?" "I'd say at least 20 years." "I remember flower beds along the west side of the house with bushes of zinnias blooming a foot tall or better every summer." "The trees in the orchard still put out bushels of lovely apples. Truth be told, I've been picking some every year for my pies and mince meat."

"You gonna tear down the house?" An elderly man at the next table turned in his chair, his watery gaze fixed on Darien. "It was grand in its day. Sure would be a shame."

Darien felt Miranda tense up across the table. "I haven't thought that far ahead," he answered. "The sellers probably won't accept the offer," he said to Miranda.

His cellphone buzzed after pie and coffee. "Darien? Stan Hale here. Congratulations! The sellers accepted! The property is all yours!"

Darien sat in stunned silence. Miranda begged him for an answer. "Was that Stan? What did he say?"

He stared at the phone in his hand. "I just bought the farm."

Darien drove back to the motel and the room he'd expected to vacate the next morning. He flopped down hard on the bed. Ivory rested her chin on his chest. Her blue eyes watched him. She seemed to sense his inner conflict. He rubbed her ears and questioned his motives out loud. "What the hell did I just do? And why the hell did I do it?"

His cellphone buzzed. "Hello, Jack. Are you sitting down? You won't believe this. I just bought an old farmhouse in the middle of bum-fuck Iowa."

Miranda

Chapter 11

Darien scrolled through email the next morning and clicked on a familiar name and address.

Eric.Lanahan@chez-nous.net

He grinned at the message attached.

Hi Chef,
News travels fast in the restaurant world. I just heard
about a five-star French restaurant that opened in Iowa.
I guessed right. Your name is all over it. Do me a favor.
Stay out of Manhattan. Just kidding. Congratulations,
Eric. BTW – What the hell are you doing in Dubuque?

Darien informed the front desk clerk of his unexpected change in planned departure. He reserved the hotel suite in Marion indefinitely and began the legal and financial process of possession and renovation of the farmhouse. Two weeks later, bundled up against the cold and with keys in hand, Darien and the McCullough sisters surveyed his unintentional investment.

"Don't you love it!" Miranda gushed. "There's so much potential here."

Her sister snorted. "There's so much work here. It's a total gut job."

Miranda frowned. "It's not that bad."

"I tend to agree with Sam," Darien interrupted. "But the good news is the inspector says the foundation is sound.

The place was treated for termites so other than a few field mice, there's no major pest problem. I've got crews coming this week to replace the wiring and plumbing and install a new furnace and central air unit. The windows are going in next week. I should be able to move in with Ivory by the end of February."

"How are you going to live in this?" Sam asked. "There's no fridge or stove." Sam pulled back and inspected the six ladder back chairs surrounding the country kitchen table. Her fingers traced a trail through years of accumulated layers of dust on the table's maple top. "There's nothing upstairs and not much down here, either."

"I'll build the kitchen first." Darien moved one of the chairs from the table and sat at a scuffed but solid oak roll top desk positioned against the wall between the front door and the cracked picture window. "As for the furniture, what's here will get me by."

"You'll need a bed," Miranda said.

"And linens," Sam added.

Darien nodded. "True enough." He stood and held the front door open for them. "Would you ladies like to go shopping?"

Miranda poked her head through the open front door of the farmhouse a few weeks later.

"Darien!" The deafening sounds of table saws, chop saws, compressors, and nails driven by hand and hydraulics drowned out her greeting. She dodged men and women in hard hats performing various specialized tasks of their professions to find Darien in the kitchen inspecting the rows of cabinets on the wall. "Hey," she said and tapped him on the shoulder to get his attention over the din. "How goes it?"

He turned his head and grinned at her. "Slow but sure," he answered.

"I see the roof and gutter guys have made an appearance."

"Yeah, they're taking advantage of the February thaw." He motioned toward the crew visible through the kitchen window at the rear of the house. "I hired a couple from Dubuque to restore and replace the wood to match the original siding. They also stabilize and rebuild sagging porches. I'll leave the front porch open as it is but I've decided to screen in the back porch."

Miranda nodded and smiled her approval. "Wow, I'm impressed. The place is really coming together. I'm so glad you're not going to slap aluminum or vinyl over the wood."

He shook his head. "No, that wouldn't look right." Darien said. "Speaking of not looking right, I'm having second thoughts about tearing down these old chestnut cabinets. They don't make them like this anymore."

Miranda's green eyes lit up. "I can refinish the wood and they'll look like new. Let me do it!"

He grinned. "Sure, go ahead," he joked, "and while you're at it see what you can do with the floor."

"I'm on it!"

His hands on her shoulders stopped her in mid hop and twirl. "Miranda, I'm kidding. I appreciate your offer to help. But there's a full wall of cabinets and at least 200 square feet of hardwood in this room. That's a big job."

The skin beneath her sweater tingled at his touch and her heart skipped a beat. *To hell with the work*, she thought. *I want to be with you!* "I like a challenge," she said instead.

Her enthusiasm briefly cheered him and for a few impulsive moments, Darien let down his guard. He cradled her flushed face in his hands and lightly brushed her lips with his thumb. She tilted her head back and he moved closer, breathed her in, felt her shiver. Miranda closed her eyes and held her breath, anticipating his kiss. The rapid rap of knuckles against the back porch doorframe dragged him back from the brink of giving in.

"Sorry!" The embarrassed workman looked away and down at his steel-toed shoes.

Darien dropped his hands to his sides and stepped away from Miranda. "No worries, man. It's all good."

Miranda held on to the kitchen counter she'd reached for to steady herself on wobbly knees. She took a deep breath and forced a smile. "I should get back to the office."

"Sure. Sure." Darien sputtered. "Maybe I'll see you and Sam at dinner."

"That would be great." Miranda spun on her heel, trotted out the front door and sprinted down the driveway to her truck. "Damn it," she muttered. She yanked open the driver's side door, hoisted herself in and slammed the door. She turned the key in the ignition without fastening her seatbelt and stomped on the gas pedal. The truck's tires spun gravel halfway to Harmony.

Chapter 12

Darien and Ivory moved into the work in progress as soon as the county inspectors declared the house habitable. With Miranda's help, the kitchen came together around refinished original cabinets and newly sanded and polished wide plank hardwood floors. Gleaming stainless steel appliances, a large apron sink and butcher block countertops chosen to complement the maple farmhouse table and chairs made the center of farmhouse family activity functional again. Miranda hummed along with the tune pumped through her ear buds and looked around for Darien. She found him in the front room watching workers install a foreign-looking retrofit in the large stone fireplace.

"What are they doing?" she asked.

"They're converting it from wood burning."

"Why?"

He shrugged. "For safety and my convenience."

Miranda inspected the unfamiliar workmanship. "Is it gas or propane?" she asked.

"Neither," he answered. "Its bio-fuel like the one Ali had installed in our apartment."

Breath caught in her throat at his mention of a woman's name. "Who?" she asked him in her best faked casual tone.

Darien stiffened and covered his mistake with an explanation. "I'd rather not chop wood."

Miranda yawned over the mail at her desk. Mornings at the veterinary clinic, afternoons working alongside Darien at the farmhouse and late nights creating works of art to sell in her studio during the approaching tourist season left precious few hours for sleep.

"You're looking tired, big sister," Sam said and massaged her sister's drooping shoulders.

"I am tired," Miranda replied. "But it's all good. I'm enjoying myself."

Sam leaned over and into her sister's line of sight, eyebrows raised above twinkling blue eyes and an impish grin. "Enjoying the work or the view?"

"What's that supposed to mean?" Miranda slid her chair away from the desk and glared at her sister.

"C'mon, Mira. Darien is a very good-looking man. I get that. But why are you putting so much sweat equity into his house?"

"There's a ton of work to be done and he needs my help. I did the same for you."

"Yeah, but I'm family," Sam poked a finger at her own chest for emphasis. "So be honest with me and with yourself." She pointed at her sister. "Is marriage your real motive?"

Anger smoldered behind Miranda's eyes. "In case you hadn't noticed, he's wearing what looks like a wedding ring on the third finger of his left hand."

"Maybe so. But I haven't seen any wife around."

Miranda calmed herself with a deep breath and a nagging memory. "He did mention someone named Ali."

Sam crossed her arms over her chest. "And?"

"He didn't say anything more and I didn't ask."

"Well, if you're interested in this guy, and I think you are, then maybe you should."

Darien would have missed his own birthday on the ninth day of May had it not been for phone calls and well wishes from his family back east. He'd let the farmhouse renovation project consume his energy and smother the smoldering loneliness. At night, the scent of lilacs blooming on a row of bushes in the backyard drifted through his bedroom window screen. He'd close his eyes, hug his pillow and for a few sweet moments he was with her. Memories of breathing in Ali's signature scent from the shampoo and shower gel she used and the lotion she wore, holding her, making love to her and the gnawing pain of losing her returned every night the lilacs bloomed.

Harmony natives and transplanted residents dropped by the farmhouse to marvel at the progress of the Meyer homestead revival. Fresh baked bread, cinnamon rolls, plates of cookies and homemade pies treated Darien and the dwindling stream of trades putting the finishing touches on the astounding transformation of the century old farmhouse.

Miranda didn't mention Ali's name or question Darien about the apparent wedding ring he wore. "Have you asked him?" Sam continued to press her sister.

 "Not yet," Miranda would say, "but I will."

"When?"

"When the time is right."

Miranda suspected her sister's motive for refusal when Sam declined Darien's invitation to dine in Cedar Rapids on a warm late spring evening. And she was right.

"You'll be alone with him. So ask him!" Sam urged.

"And what am I going to say," Miranda hissed. "Darien, I know this is really none of my business. But before I fall totally in love with you, I need to know if you're married."

"That's a bit direct. But at least you'll have your answer."

Probably not the one I'm hoping for, Miranda thought.

The Range Rover arrived at Miranda's combined art studio and adjacent efficiency apartment promptly at seven. She tugged at the wrinkles in the skirt of the only dress she owned and frowned at the loose fit and plainness of its pale blue cotton.

Darien got out and opened the passenger's side car door for her. The nearness of him, the scent and style of him, made Miranda's hands tremble. His black slacks hung to pressed perfection from the black leather belt around his trim waist to the tops of his polished black leather dress shoes. The open buttons at his neck, rolled up sleeves on muscular arms and broad chest beneath the fitted garnet red shirt suggested a sensuous side to him she longed to discover.

Darien provided a detailed progress report on the homestead project during the drive to Cedar Rapids. Miranda heard only scattered words through the questions in her head that she tried and failed to push past her lips. He parked the car in front of a sandstone store front where a glowing red neon sign behind tinted glass announced the shiny red front door was Open.

"This is it." He got out and walked around the hood of the car to open the door for her again.

"Where are we?" She took the hand he offered and stepped over the curb.

"We are at one of the restaurants I helped open. Have you ever had sushi?"

She wrinkled her nose. "Isn't that raw fish?"

"Not all sushi has raw fish. That's sashimi. Sushi is mostly rice, seaweed, and vegetables." He smiled at her sideways glance of doubt. "Trust me."

"Chef Darien!" A short, pudgy man in a dark grey linen suit greeted them at the door. "Long time no see, stranger!"

"How's business, Bernie?"

"Couldn't be better. No complaints." Bernie reached behind the slick black lacquer reception stand near the door and pulled out a pair of menus. "Who is this lovely lady?" His deep set brown eyes twinkled above round, ruddy cheeks.

"This is my friend Miranda. She's been helping me with a project and I'm treating her to a night out," Darien replied. "Bernie owns this place and the French restaurant in Dubuque," he explained to her.

"Where I get rave reviews from customers every night. Best chateaubriand this side of Chicago." Bernie led them through the dining room to a secluded table bathed in soft ambient light. He pulled out a chair for Miranda and winked at Darien. "Enjoy."

The waiter appeared within minutes of Bernie's departure. Darien ordered miso soup for two and sushi selections within Miranda's culinary comfort zone.

"What's this?" She spooned green paste into a small white bowl.

"Wasabi. Here," he said, reached for and handed her a pint-sized glass bottle. "Mix it with soy sauce. But go light on that. It's hot."

"I've eaten homemade salsa by the spoonful," she bragged. "Besides, it's green, not red." She dipped the rolled up rice, cucumber, and avocado California roll into a lump of wasabi swimming in brown liquid and plopped the sushi onto her tongue. Darien waited for the expected red-faced reaction. He threw his head back, laughed out loud, and handed her his full glass of water after she'd drained hers.

She dabbed at her watering eyes with a napkin and laughed at herself. "That was painful. But it was worth it."

"How so?"

"That's the first time I've heard you laugh."

Chapter 13

Darien walked through and inspected his renovated house in the late afternoon of the first full day without contractors and crew. A light breeze carried the scent of sweet autumn clematis through the back porch screens. The kitchen he'd designed blended original charm with modern necessity and the two-piece powder room nestled under the stairs added main floor convenience. Reclaimed hardwood floors and finishes reflected natural light in the four bedrooms upstairs. He relished the luxury of tepid water gently pulsing from angled shower jets in the upstairs four-piece bath. The central air unit clicked on to comply with the thermostat setting he chose and flames flared and disappeared in the front room fireplace at his remote command. He paced the length of the sturdy front porch that no longer sagged and admired the landscaper's design and installation that had transformed the once barren front lawn into lush green grass and shrubs and vibrant beds of perennial and annual colors.

He sat at the old roll top desk and hummed to himself as he sifted through invoices and receipts. His feeling of accomplishment faded to bitter despair when he checked the time and noticed the date on his wristwatch.

One year ago today I lost the love of my life. The thought pierced his soul.

His shaking hands scattered the pile of papers to the floor. His eyes saw only her. His ears heard her voice. He reached out for her but the arms that pulled her to him were empty. He fell to his knees, hugged his ribs and struggled for air between wrenching sobs delayed and suppressed since the violent collision that killed his joy. He felt the scratch of Ivory's tongue lapping at streams of unleashed tears on his cheeks. He buried his face in her fur and wept. Total exhaustion eventually conquered his emotional agony in the darkness of fallen night. He closed his eyes against the world without her and slept on the hardwood floor beside the vigilant Husky.

"C'mon, D, answer the phone, damn it!" Jack McKenna had been trying to reach his younger brother since the anniversary of Ali's fatal accident the day before. He'd paced the floor through a sleepless night and packed a suitcase at dawn. "Hey, Beth," he called to his wife. "Do you remember the name of that jerkwater town in Iowa where Darien bought a farmhouse?"

Beth poked her head around the door frame between their kitchen and dining room. "I think he said Harmony."

"Yeah, that's it." Jack searched the internet for government and business phone listings in Harmony, Iowa and found the name and phone number of the town's veterinarian. "I'll try here first," he muttered to himself. He called the office of Samantha McCullough DVM. Miranda answered. "This is Jack McKenna. I'm in New Jersey and I've been trying to call my brother Darien. He told me he brings his dog to the only veterinarian in town and I guess you're it."

"That's my sister Samantha. I'm Miranda. How can I help you?"

"Do you know my brother? Has he been in the office? Have you seen him around town?"

"Yes, I know Darien and no, I haven't seen him lately. If he's not answering his phone, I could go out to his farmhouse and check on him."

"Would you, please? And tell him to call me."

Miranda's attempts at reaching Darien by phone were no more successful than Jack's. She logged out of the office computer and slung the strap of her purse over her shoulder. "Sam, I'm going out to Darien's place. I'll meet you at Hank's at five."

Miranda cranked the complaining engine on her high-mileage pickup truck and drove the 12-mile distance to Darien's driveway. She parked behind the Range Rover and took a moment to remember the before and admire the after, from the green shingles on the roof to the flawless white pillars on the porch. She climbed the porch steps and knocked once, twice, three times at the front door.

No response.

She cupped her hands and peered through the front bay window panes. "Darien?" She spotted the overturned chair at the empty desk and the papers that littered the floor.

She stepped off the porch and trotted past the blooming beds of bright yellow zinnia and unfurled pink four o'clock blossoms along the side of the house. The door to the screened-in back porch was unlocked. She called to him again and banged her knuckles against the locked back door.

Nothing.

Worry quickened her pace and breathing. She circled back to the front porch and started to punch 911 into her cellphone when the front door opened.

"Hey, I was about to call for help." Concern quickly replaced relief. Darien had not shaved or otherwise groomed himself in days and his wrinkled polo shirt and cargo pants looked like he'd slept in them as long. His eyes were bloodshot and the skin above the dark stubble was mottled red. He looked like he'd been crying. "Are you OK?" she asked.

He cleared his throat. "I haven't been feeling well," he said.

"Do you need a doctor?" He shook his head. "Can I bring you anything?"

"No. Miranda, I just want to be left alone."

"Oh." She straightened and backed away from him. "Well, you know where to find me if you change your mind." She turned on her heel, quick-stepped off the porch, and turned back when she remembered the message she'd come to deliver. "Call your brother. He's worried about you." She got in her truck, revved the cranky engine and drove back into town.

Darien stepped through the veterinary clinic door at mid-day. Miranda noticed and told him that he looked much better than he had three long days before.

"Thanks," he said. "Are you free for lunch?"

"I'll grab my purse and be right with you." They crossed the street to Hank's Longhorn Café. He pulled out a chair for her at a far corner table and sat across from her.

"Thank you for driving out to check on me."

"No problem." She waited, hoping he'd confide in her.

He ran his fingers through his hair and sat back. "I had a rough few days. But that's no excuse for being rude. I apologize. And I'd like to make it up to you." He leaned forward. She held her breath. "How about we break in my new kitchen?"

She smiled. "Are you inviting me to dinner at your place, chef?"

118

He smiled back. "That's the general idea."

She laughed. "Well it's about time! And your timing is perfect. We've got something to celebrate." Her emerald green eyes shone above creamy skin tinged pale pink with excitement.

So beautiful, he thought.

"I sold a painting!" she said.

"You did! When?"

"Yesterday. A couple from the Twin Cities stopped in my studio, loved my work, and bought my water lily landscape. They paid full price! And they commissioned another watercolor of a photo they'd taken on their way down from Minnesota through Spirit Lake! They gave me a $500 advance! Isn't that fantastic!" Darien envied her joy. He reached across the table and squeezed her hand. "I'm happy for you," he said.

The lightning bolt reaction to his touch coursed up her arm and exploded in her core. She crossed her legs to control the heat.

"Saturday night at seven?" he asked.

She squeezed his hand and nodded. "I'll be there."

Chapter 14

Darien planned a meticulous menu as though his emotional recovery depended on it. He scoured the markets in Iowa City for ingredients and the necessary equipment to satisfy his therapeutic need to create a three course culinary masterpiece with lemon sorbet intermezzo. His expert eye scanned rows of bottled wine at John's Market for the perfect pairing to serve with dinner.

Miranda picked through her inadequate wardrobe and sighed. She closed her closet door in disgust, climbed in her pickup, and headed down the highway. She blew past the intended outlet shops destination and continued west on I-80 to the fashion possibilities of the state's capitol and largest city.

Darien moved around his kitchen with chef's precision, using every skill and technique in his culinary arsenal. Dinner was well in hand when Miranda knocked at his front door. "C'mon in," he called to her.

She opened the screen door and stepped into the sparsely furnished living room. The heels of her famous maker skinny-strap gold sandals rapped the hardwood floor. She walked the perimeter of the large oval area rug in front of the fireplace, patted the sleeping white dog curled up between a pair of plump floor pillows, and followed the tempting aroma to the kitchen. Her heart skipped a beat at the sensual sight of the man handling the whisk.

 The polo shirt hugging his broad chest and sculpted abs was as black as his hair and the sexy five-o'clock shadow on his face and neck. The muscles in his strong arms rippled with every expert move between the six-burner stove and butcher block-topped island at the kitchen's center. His steel grey eyes focused on every detail and the ties of the apron around his waist dangled over the part of him that Miranda longed to touch.

"If dinner tastes even half as good as it smells, I can't wait to dive in." She hoisted the department store shopping bag from her hands to the counter and covered the old wooden table with its contents, spreading a white linen tablecloth and pressing long white taper candles into brushed pewter candlestick holders. She filled the glass vase she'd found on the store's bargain table with tap water from the sink and a bouquet of pink and white carnations. "What's on the menu, chef?"

"That's a secret until it's served," he said. He turned from the simmering pots on the stove and almost didn't recognize her. High-heeled sandals accentuated long, sleek legs uncovered by slits from the ankle-length hem to the knee of her mint green sleeveless dress. The V-neckline and shimmery, taut material revealed round, full breasts Darien had not noticed before. Her copper-colored hair, usually pulled back into a long braid or puffy chignon, flowed unbound over her shoulders and down her back to her waist. A pale shade of pink blushed her high cheekbones and lush, full lips.

He swallowed hard before he spoke. "New dress?"

She smiled and blushed. "And shoes. And a few festive touches for the table." She set the vase of flowers between the candles. "Need any help?"

He forced himself to look away and concentrate on dinner. He drank the last of the butter-colored chardonnay from a glass he'd filled more than once during preparation. "You can pour yourself wine." He slid a wine glass from the rack below the cupboard and set it next to the open half-empty bottle on the counter.

"Oh, I almost forgot." She reached into the bag for the bottle she couldn't afford but had hoped would impress him. "I really don't know much about wine. The clerk recommended it." She handed the bottle to him.

Darien read the label of a lower end chenin blanc than he would choose but one he knew exceeded her budget. "We'll save this for later," he said and stowed the bottle in the fridge. "White wine is best when chilled."

"There must be something else I can do."

"Nope. I'm plating it," he said, and pulled a chair out for her.

Delicate hearts of palm lay in a bed of thinly-sliced fennel seasoned with balsamic vinegar and extra virgin olive oil. Risotto complimented main course caramelized Iowa pork and cranberries prepared to perfection in a balsamic reduction. Amaretto accompanied velvety zabiglione served with fresh strawberries. Wine flowed through the courses.

Darien delighted in Miranda's exaggerated yet sincere expressions of pure pleasure. He introduced her to the flavor enhancing trick of biting into a strawberry, sprinkling the bitten part with ground pepper, and laying the strawberry on her tongue pepper-side down. He laughed at her wide-eyed astonishment and eager entreaty to "do that again."

Daylight dissolved to soft, warm darkness lit by the glow of candles and recessed pot lights. Miranda swirled and drank the last of the wine in her glass. "I have never enjoyed a meal more or eaten that much at one time ever and I don't regret one bite."

Darien sat back and admired his dinner guest. *God, she's beautiful, he thought.* "Would you like anything else?" he asked her.

Yes, she thought, but we probably won't go there. "Maybe a cup of extra strong coffee for the drive home."

Darien looked at her flushed face and grinned. "I don't think driving back into town is an option."

She grinned back. "What are you suggesting?"

"Nothing that a gentleman wouldn't offer. You may sleep in my bed."

Her grin widened. "And where will you sleep?"

"On the rug and pillows by the fireplace."

"That doesn't sound very comfortable."

He didn't want to tell her he'd recently spent a few nights on the floor. "I'll manage," he said.

Miranda kicked off her sandals, pushed back from the table and stood on unsteady bare feet. "Then let's tuck you in."

Darien blew out the candles, followed her into the living room, and ignited the dancing bio-fuel in the fireplace. Miranda sat on the rug, hugged her knees and patted the floor pillow next to the one nestled at her back. Darien settled on the rug beside her.

"This is nice." Miranda stretched her toes toward the flame and rolled on her side to face him. Her lips were inches from his, her breasts within his reach.

"Yes, it is," he agreed. The hunger within him simmered and boiled in a visceral cauldron stoked by wine and fueled by desire. *Oh God, the voice in his head groaned. I want to feel good again.*

"I haven't enjoyed myself this much in a long time," she said.

"Neither have I," he responded.

"Thank you for a fabulous dinner, Darien."

I want to be with a woman again, the voice in his head screamed. I want to taste her, touch her, feel her in my arms! "My pleasure." Their lips came together in a sizzling press of passion.

He coiled his fingers into the thick luxury of her hair and parted her lips with his tongue. She lay back on the pillow. Her fingers caressed the nape of his neck, moved to his shoulders and pushed under his shirt to touch the damp skin along his spine. He kissed her long exposed neck from her chin to the sweet softness above the V-neckline of her dress. He stretched the compliant straps from her shoulders and traced the curves above and the dip between her breasts with the tip of his tongue. His hands burrowed beneath thin cloth and a lace bra and his fingers fondled the nipples that rose at his touch. He stroked the length of her with his palms, found the slits in the material gathered at her knees and guided her dress up the smooth softness of her thighs. He stopped at her panties and waited for signs of resistance.

"Darien," she whispered, and pulled at his belt buckle. He undid his belt, rolled onto his back, and let her open the button, the zipper and have her way with his sex now exposed. She stroked him softly with her fingertips, her nails teasing the sensitive tip of his penis, her lips kissing him up and down the shaft, her tongue circling the tracks of her kiss. He groaned and reached for her, pushing her panties aside to rub the engorged spot under his thumb. She rolled on her back and slid soaked panties past her ankles. With his fingers inside her, he licked the glistening juices coating her inner thighs.

She cried out. "Please, Darien!"

He opened her legs wide with the palms of his hands on her thighs. She shuddered when his lips closed around her and his tongue probed her. He groaned and drank her ample arousal.

She clawed at his shoulders. "Please, Darien!" she repeated.

"Do you want me inside you, Miranda?"

"Yes!"

He covered her, drove into her, deeper as her legs wrapped around him, faster with her rocking movements that implored him. He prolonged his release until he felt her quiver and clench around him and he could hold back no more.

Darien awoke to a chorus of crickets and cicadas and the feel of a woman beside him. He opened his eyes, saw the mound of copper-colored hair on the pillow next to his, and stifled a groan.

He remembered helping Miranda to her feet and following her up the stairs to lay naked with her in his bed. There was no further need for discretion or restraint. He moved with the rhythm of their lovemaking, pressed his body to and into hers and savored the abundance that flowed from her. He let himself be tamed by her knees at his hips and entranced by the hypnotic pendulum swing of her long hair as she rode them both to climax. Her supple body wrapped him in positions he'd imagined but never tried. He entered her again and again in the moonlit hours like a ravenous man released from solitary confinement.

He inched away from her in the early light of dawn, careful not to wake her and risk words he was not ready to hear or say. He tiptoed downstairs and dressed in yesterday's clothes strewn on the living room floor. He opened the back porch screen door and let Ivory out into the humid mist of late summer morning.

Darien dropped into the webbed seat of a steel-framed lawn chair he'd found spooning with its mate in the farmhouse basement and held his aching head in his hands. *You ass, he muttered to himself. You really outdid yourself this time.*

He rehearsed every excuse, reason and apology he could think of to soften the blow. But he knew Miranda deserved the truth. Wallowing in depression and self-pity had made him vulnerable, reopened a cavernous wound, and shredded his personal code of decency. He had betrayed Ali *"I will forever and always be your wife,"* he heard her say. And he'd lied to a friend. He despised himself for what he had done and failed to do and what he now would have to do. The crickets and cicadas in the surrounding trees and field scolded him. Birds announcing the approach of day accused him. He confessed his sin but forgiveness eluded him in the harsh reality of morning.

"Penny for them." Miranda stood in front of him. "I hope you don't mind." She was wearing his robe. He glanced up and shook his head. She sat in the lawn chair next to his and stroked his bare forearm with her fingertips. "Not a morning person? Or are you just not yourself until you've had a cup of coffee."

He patted her hand softly and sat back in the lawn chair. "Miranda, I need to tell you how I ended up in Iowa." He took a deep breath and precious time to compose the details of his life with and after Ali. "I was the executive chef at a restaurant in Manhattan when I met the love of my life."

"Ali," Miranda said. Surprise broke through his shame. He blinked hard and searched her eyes for an answer. "You mentioned her name when the workmen were putting in the fireplace. You said it was bio-fuel like the one Ali had installed in your apartment."

"Oh," he said. "You picked up on that." She nodded and he continued. "It was love at first sight for me. Ali was twenty years older. But that didn't matter. I moved in with her the day before New Year's Eve. We got engaged on Valentine's Day and were married in August. Ali owned a media consulting firm in Brooklyn. I resigned as chef to have more time with my wife and started my own consulting business renovating and opening new restaurants. The same type of work I did at the restaurants here." He paused and looked out over the vanishing mist. "Ali and I had … an amazing eight years together."

His voice trailed off. Miranda was curious to know why he spoke about her in the past tense. But she waited for him to begin again. "We planned to retire together before our wedding anniversary. I bought two open return plane tickets that would take us to all the places we had promised to share with each other, starting with a second honeymoon in Paris. The day before we were going to board that plane, Ali's car was hit head on by a drunk driver. She was on her way back to Brooklyn from her last appointment with a client." His shoulders slumped. He rubbed his forehead. "I didn't even get to say goodbye."

The lump in Miranda's throat kept her from saying anything at first. A warbling goldfinch in the apple orchard split the silence. "Darien, I'm so …"

He cut her off with a wave of his hand. "Don't say it. I've heard it enough." He shifted in the lawn chair. "I lost Ali a year ago. I hung around the apartment for weeks in total denial. I guess I kept waiting for her to come home. Then I ran away. I bought the Range Rover and headed west. I had no idea where I was going. I stopped in Iowa for no particular reason. You know the rest." He moved his chair around to face her. Their knees touched. His hands reached out for hers. She laid her palms into his.

"Miranda, I don't regret last night unless it ends our friendship. You mean so much to me."

"As a friend," she said.

"I never intended to lead you on or hurt you. I'm just not ready. I can't give you more right now." He squeezed her hands. "I hope you understand."

She looked down at their hands, slowly pulled hers away and folded them in her lap. "I'll get my clothes and give you back your robe."

He followed her into the kitchen. "At least let me make you breakfast." he pleaded.

When she turned back to him, the hurt he saw in her eyes felt like a punch to his gut. "That's OK. Sam's probably wondering what happened to me." She gathered up her clothes, used the downstairs powder room to change, handed him his robe and walked out the front door. He watched her pickup truck until the red running lights disappeared in the dust kicked up by tires on the gravel road.

Truth and Consequences

Chapter 15

"That's a likely story." Sam sat with her arms crossed over her chest.

"You think he made it up," Miranda challenged her.

"Sorry, but it sounds too much like a plot from a bad movie script."

Miranda sped from Darien's driveway to her sister's front door. Sam teased her at first for her morning-after appearance in the dress Miranda had taken a day trip to Des Moines to find. The joking stopped with Miranda's roller coaster ride of emotions, from the anticipation and exhilaration of the night before to anger and tears in the painful reality of morning.

"If I could believe he lied, then I could hate him," Miranda said. "But I feel so bad for him. What if he is telling the truth, Sam?"

"There's one way to find out." Sam sat in front of her open laptop at the dining room table and nudged the mouse that flared the screen to life.

"What are you going to do?"

"Google him."

Miranda shook her head. "I don't want to do that. It's like we're invading his privacy."

"Oh, like he didn't invade yours?"

"Ha, ha." Miranda peered over her sister's shoulder and studied the search engine results. Sam began to sift through the links matching Darien's name.

"Well, looks like he was telling the truth about being an executive chef in Manhattan." Sam whistled. "Wow! He was a hottie! He even had his own cooking show."

Miranda was more interested in the words than the photos, although she had to admit Sam was right. She sighed at the image of the younger, dashing, and extraordinarily handsome Darien in chef whites. "He told me he left Chez Nous to spend more time with Ali. Click on this link." She pointed to a New York Times story about the city's revised building code guidelines for 500-year storms following Hurricane Sandy's devastation. Darien's work on a disaster plan task force had changed the way New York restaurants operated. Basement prep kitchens were moved upstairs, seating was moved downstairs and buildings were retrofitted with waterproof materials to more efficiently drain and pump out water. Another article announced Darien's appointment to the consulting team overseeing the opening of the new 1 World Trade Center restaurant on the 101st floor.

"Enough about him," Sam said. "Let's find out if he really had a wife." She typed 'Ali McKenna' with no results.

"Ali is probably short for Alison. Try that," Miranda urged.

"No results for Alison with one L or two," Sam said. "I hate to say I told you so."

Miranda wasn't ready to give up. "Darien said she owned a media consulting firm in Brooklyn. Maybe it's still there."

Sam asked the search engine to find media consulting firms in Brooklyn, New York. "There's not too many listed." She clicked on and scrolled down the Clarke Media Consultants website home page. "This can't be it. Clarke Media Consultants is owned by Mimi Teague and Kenneth Wong. I'll try the next one."

"Wait," Miranda said. "Click on About Us." Sam's cursor and mouse click revealed the photo and bio of founder Alison Clarke McKenna. The two women stared at the portrait of the sophisticated older woman with dark brown eyes and a confident smile. "She was beautiful," Miranda said.

"New York Times editor, Pulitzer Prize winner," Sam read. "The bio only mentions her credentials." Sam returned to the search engine.

"What are you looking for now?" Miranda asked.

"Her obituary." Sam called up the New York Times archives and found Ali's photo again. "Alison Clarke McKenna, Pulitzer Prize-winning journalist, former New York Times editor, founder of Clarke Media Consultants and beloved wife of Chef Darien McKenna, was pronounced dead on arrival at Good Samaritan Hospital on Long Island from injuries suffered in a two-vehicle accident .."

"I've seen enough." Miranda pulled out and dropped into a chair at the table. Sam closed her laptop. The sisters sat in stunned silence.

Sam squeezed Miranda's hand. "I'm still pissed that he hurt you. But now I feel bad for him, too," she said.

Darien's good reason to feel bad kept him away from Miranda. He'd enter all but the last digit of her phone number on his cellphone then cancel the call. He drove toward town to see her. But guilt turned him back. Disgusted with himself and deeply depressed, he packed for a road trip, locked up the farmhouse and set out for a pet-friendly rental in Door County he'd discovered and reserved online. Blue sky mornings, afternoons cleansed by rain showers and nights wrapped in a thick blanket of night sky stars he'd viewed from his Iowa backyard but never seen in the city passed uncounted and unencumbered. The cellphone he'd silenced in the deep woods cottage on a private beach buzzed to life as he piloted the Range Rover along a four-lane highway north of Green Bay.

"Where the hell have you been?" Jack's irritation and anxiety came through loud and clear from New Jersey.

"I'm on the road. I'll call you when I get to the next rest stop." Darien pulled off and parked, staked Ivory's leash alongside the picnic table she promptly got underneath, and called his brother.

"I've been trying to find you for three weeks!"

Darien checked the date on the watch he hadn't worn for awhile. "I'm sorry, Jack. I didn't realize I'd been out of touch that long. I guess signals are weak in Wisconsin," he lied.

"Apparently! What are you doing in Wisconsin?"

"I … needed to get away for awhile."

"How could you get any farther away from civilization than Iowa?"

I keep trying, he thought. "What did I miss? Is something wrong?"

"No, nothing's wrong and you haven't missed anything yet. The honor of your presence is requested in November for Hannah's graduation from NYU and at her wedding in December."

"What?! I thought she was graduating next May."

"Well, she quit her job and doubled her course load so she could graduate early, get married and move to Australia with her new husband."

Darien whistled through his teeth. "Man, am I glad I got off the road to hear this."

"You're not half as stunned as we are. Beth is in frantic mode planning a graduation party and a wedding."

"No worries. She'll pull it off," Darien said, remembering his sister-in-law's clipboard and check marks on the meticulous 'to-do' list of tasks that planned the perfect wedding day for him and Ali. "What's this about Australia?"

"Yeah, that's the part that's tearing me up. My baby girl is moving half way around the world. Evan got a job offer in Sydney he couldn't refuse."

"Is Evan that zit-faced kid with the glasses she dated in high school?"

Jack laughed. "Yep, same kid. Only he's not so zit-faced anymore and he wears contacts. He's a good guy. Graduated with honors from MIT. He loves her and she's crazy about him. They're getting married the Saturday before Christmas."

"I can't believe little Hannah is all grown up."

"Me either." Silent seconds ticked by until Jack spoke again. "D, you've been gone almost a year. Come home. We miss you. I miss you."

Darien sighed. He knew the time had come. He had to go back and face the life and loss he'd left behind. "You know I'll be there for Hannah. I'll call you when I get back to the farmhouse."

Darien called Stan the real estate man the next day.

"The old girl looks fantastic!" Stan proclaimed. "The hardwood floors and the brand spanking new kitchen and bath will sell her for sure. The powder room and screened-in back porch are nice touches, too." Stan sang the praises of the new furnace and central air unit and the tidy condition of the basement but changed his tune when he saw the debris in the barn. "Maybe potential buyers won't look in the barn. They might just raze it and build a garage."

"It looks bad, I know," Darien admitted. "Give me a week. I'll get this stuff hauled away before the first open house."

Stan flashed his best salesman-of-the-century smile. "Great! Then just leave it to me. I'll get you a solid offer and top dollar."

Chapter 16

Sam wiped her hands on the cleanest towel she could find on the backseat of her rusty but reliable four-wheel drive red pickup truck with the gray flatbed topper. She bounced out of the driver's seat and through the front door of Miranda's art studio and gallery. The tinkling silver bell over the door announced her arrival.

"I just spent six hours coaxing a calf out of a cow and I've got to pee."

Miranda looked up from the brush coloring the cold press watercolor paper taped to the table in front of her. "Go ahead. The door's open."

Sam entered Miranda's living space and hung a sharp left into the tiny bathroom. She noticed the wastebasket at her knees filled with several opened and discarded pharmacy boxes of used home pregnancy tests.

Sam marched across the wide planks of the studio's hardwood floor and stood in front of her sister. "Is there something you'd like to tell me?" she asked.

"Like what?"

"Like why you're sweating a late period?"

Miranda stopped painting and dropped her brush in the water cup. "I thought you were going to use my bathroom, not snoop around in it."

Sam's hands went to her hips and her eyes narrowed.

"C'mon, Mira. Talk to me."

Miranda rubbed her closed eyes and sighed. "I'm pretty sure I'm pregnant."

"How sure?"

"Well, you saw. Six positive home pregnancy tests can't all be wrong."

"How far along are you?"

"Six weeks and five days, considering I know the date of conception."

"So Darien is the father?"

Miranda's face flushed in anger. "Of course the baby is Darien's!"

"OK, OK, don't get hot."

"You shouldn't have had to ask."

"You're right. I'm sorry. I'm just shocked that neither of you used protection."

"I didn't expect to be expecting. I told you before. We got caught up in the moment without thinking about the possible consequences."

"Have you informed him of the consequences?"

Miranda shook her head. "I wanted to tell him before anyone else, even you. But I needed to be sure first."

"Have you seen a doctor?"

"Not yet."

"What are you waiting for?"

She looked down at her hands now folded in her lap. "An answer to a prayer that isn't going to happen." Tears of fear pooled in Miranda's eyes. "Oh, Sam. I don't know what he'll say or worse yet not say."

"Well, don't assume the worst. He said he wasn't ready right now. Maybe finding out he's going to be a father will push him toward ready."

"The last thing I want is for him to marry me out of some sense of moral duty or financial obligation."

"Mira, you know I'll help you as much as I can. But you don't have the money to raise a child alone. Besides, he should take that responsibility and I'm sure he will. Darien may be a jerk but he's not a total asshole. So when are you going to tell him?"

"I've got an appointment with Doctor Gregson tomorrow. When I know for sure, I'll tell him."

Darien answered after the third ring tone. "Hello?"

"Hi, Darien. It's Miranda."

The flood of relief and elation at the sound of her voice surprised him. "I've been meaning to call you. How have you been?"

"OK."

"How's Sam?"

"Fine. Are you busy?"

"Not anymore. I finally got all the junk out of the barn. I'm just about done packing up for a trip back east."

"Oh," was all she could say.

"I'd like to see you before I go."

"When are you leaving?"

"Tomorrow."

"How long will you be gone?"

After a long pause, he stammered out an answer. "I'm … n-not sure. Can I meet you in town? Or maybe we could go to dinner in Iowa City."

"I can come out to the farmhouse this afternoon, if that's OK."

"Sure."

Miranda felt her pulse racing the closer she got to the farmhouse. Standing on the front porch, he looked larger than life and even more handsome than she remembered.

"Good to see you," he said, and held the screen door open for her. She started to tremble when she saw the cardboard boxes and suitcases stacked in the middle of the room.

"What's all this?" she asked.

"Miranda …" he stepped toward her. "I wanted to tell you before you heard it from someone else. I've put the farmhouse up for sale." She spun around to confront him with the truth they both knew.

"You're not coming back, are you?"

His jaw set. "No. I'm not."

Her sensitive stomach threatened to empty its contents and her knees refused to hold her up. He caught her as the room around her began to spin.

"Miranda!" He guided her safely to a chair at the kitchen table and filled a glass of water that she refused.

"Thanks, but that probably won't stay down right now."

The concern on his face was very real. "Have you been sick?"

"Every morning and most nights for weeks. Darien, I'm pregnant."

He dropped into the chair across from hers and his back and shoulders hit the ladder back with an audible thump. He stared at her. His grey eyes revealed nothing of the response brewing behind them. *Say something! she screamed in her head.* He broke the agonizing silence with an emotionless yet predictable question. "Are you sure?"

"Confirmed by a doctor after a half dozen positive home pregnancy tests, so yes, I'm sure." Jumbled thoughts held in check for weeks rushed past her lips. "I'm not going to make excuses or place blame. We're way past that. I considered adoption. But I can't see myself going there. And I am absolutely NOT getting an abortion."

"Of course not," he said. His quick agreeable response began to lift the burden she'd carried alone.

"Darien, I can't raise this child selling art to tourists."

"I wouldn't expect you to." He reached into his pants pocket for his wallet. "I don't have much cash on me. But what I've got should help. I'll send more when I get back to New York."

"You're moving back?" Miranda tried hard to ease the anxiety from her voice.

"My niece is graduating from college at mid-term and getting married before Christmas. She's moving to Australia with her husband after the holidays. I would have gone back this year anyway even without a wedding. My folks aren't getting any younger and I miss my family."

"I'm sure they miss you, too."

"Miranda, I promise I won't abandon you." She bit her lip to hold off tears. "If you want a legal agreement drawn up for child support, I'll pay … "

She pushed back from the table and stood to go. "I'm sure we'll work something out."

He followed her to the front door. "Are you feeling well enough to drive? Let me lock up and follow you back into town."

"I'll be fine." She started down the porch steps.

"Wait!" he called and returned with the cash she'd left behind on the table. "Please take this, Miranda," he said and pressed the folded bills into her hand. "I'll be staying at my brother's house through the holidays. I'll give you his phone number."

"I have it. He gave it to me when he couldn't find you."

"Oh, right. Call me there if you can't reach me on my cell."

She nodded. "Well, I guess we've said all we need to say. Have a safe trip." She walked away from him, head held high in a show of strength she did not feel.

Miranda collapsed into Sam's arms and sobbed.

"Oh my God! What did that bastard say to you? That he's had a vasectomy and can't be the father?!"

Miranda sputtered out a laugh that cut through the tears. "No, he didn't deny paternity. And he's not a bastard." Miranda opened her clenched hand and unfolded the clammy wad of bills Darien had given her. "He insisted I take this and said he'd send more when he gets back to New York."

"New York!"

"Yes, Sam. New York. He's going home." Miranda sagged into a waiting room chair in the empty after-hours veterinary clinic. "He's packed up and stacked everything mobile that he owns in the middle of the front room and put the farmhouse up for sale."

Sam sat in the chair beside her. "He just found out about the baby. He could change his mind."

Miranda shook her head. "You don't get it, Sam. He's going back to the life he knows with his family in the big city where he lived with her. I can't possibly compete with that glamour much less a ghost! Oh, he said he wouldn't abandon me. Me! Just me, Sam! He never mentioned the baby, except when he offered to pay the legal fees to draw up a mutually satisfactory agreement for child support."

"Well. At least you'll have the money to raise my niece or nephew."

Miranda buried her damp, tear-stained face in her hands. "I need his money. But I want him."

Chapter 17

Darien left before sunrise the next morning. He'd packed the car the night before, tossed one last fitful night on the bare mattress with a pillow to support his lower back on the long drive to New Jersey and a blanket to cover the passenger's seat for Ivory. He wanted to distance himself from Iowa as quickly as the legal speed limits would allow. He logged 15 straight hours on the road, stopping only for quick meals, bathroom breaks and to walk his dog. He called his brother from the first rest stop inside the state of New Jersey.

"Jack? It's Darien."

"Hey, man. Where are you?"

"New Jersey. I'll be pulling into your driveway in an hour or so, give or take with traffic."

"We weren't expecting you until tomorrow."

"If it's a problem, I can find a motel."

"Are you kidding me? Beth has had the guest room ready for days. We even bought a bag of food for Ivory."

"I hope you have beer. I really need a cold one, bro."

"The fridge is stocked with brews and corned beef from the deli."

"Man, I forgot how much I missed that. And you."

"See you soon. Drive safe, D."

Two hours later, with the packed SUV parked in his brother's locked garage, Darien finished his second beer and kosher corned beef on rye. Ivory licked up the last bit of beef gravy Beth had poured over her bowl of crunchy kibble and sat, contented and watchful at her master's side.

"She has lovely eyes," Beth observed.

"More like spooky," Jack said over the rim of his empty beer glass.

Darien rubbed his dog's ears. "You'll get used to it sooner than she gets used to you."

"You got her from an animal shelter?" Nathan asked his uncle.

"A humane society, if you can call it that. They were going to put her down because some self-appointed executioner said she was a bite risk. Ivory doesn't have a mean bone in her body. The most aggressive behavior I've seen is like she is now, when she stares you down. That can be intimidating. She talks sometimes, like she's trying to tell me something. But I've never heard her growl."

"Can I pet her?" Nathan asked.

"I'm not sure she's ready for that yet. Let her come to you."

"Hello, Ivory," Nathan said. "You're a pretty girl," and he held his closed hand out to her.

Ivory shifted her intense blue-eyed gaze to Nathan. Without hesitation, the Husky went to him and laid her chin on his knee.

"Well, I'll be damned," Darien said. "I've never seen her do that. Except with me."

Nathan smiled down at the dog and ran his fingers through her fur. "She likes me." Ivory licked Nathan's other hand as if to confirm their new friendship.

Darien stretched and yawned. "I hate to break this up. But I'm beat. I'll probably sleep all day tomorrow."

"As long as you're ready for dinner with the folks here tomorrow night," Jack said.

"Wake me up an hour before so I can shower and shave," Darien joked.

"You got it," Jack said and patted his brother's shoulder. "It's good to have you home, D."

Darien wrapped his arm around his brother's neck. "It's good to be back." When he stood, Ivory followed. "C'mon, girl." The white dog ambled after him down the split-level home's hallway to the shared comfort of crisp sheets, down-filled pillows and a soft blanket.

Darien rubbed his eyes open and sighed with relief. He knew where he was and could almost believe the farmhouse, Miranda and the baby he had made with her were only the setting, plot and characters in a dream during his long and restful night's sleep. He tossed off the blanket and sat on the edge of the guest room bed. The angle of sunlight peeking through thin slits in the window blinds hinted at mid-afternoon. The suitcase from the SUV stood upright inside the door. He snapped it open, slipped on a clean pair of jeans and white t-shirt pulled from it, and strolled down the hallway.

"Hey, D, I was just about to bang on your door and drag your sorry butt into the shower." Jack grinned at him over the pile of students' papers on the dining room table.

"I need a cup of coffee first." Darien crossed into the adjacent galley-style kitchen and took a cup from the mug tree next to the half-full glass carafe on the drip machine's hot plate.

"Better make it quick. Mom and Dad are on their way here from Hoboken."

"Is it that late? You said they were coming for dinner." Darien jumped at the sound of the slamming back door. Ivory ran in ahead of Nathan to Darien's side, the leash trailing behind her.

Nathan grinned. "We had the best walk ever."

Darien scratched her behind the ears. "Thanks for looking after her for me."

Nathan shrugged and opened the refrigerator door. "No problem. She's a great dog."

"Nathan! You had lunch an hour ago!" Beth's voice carried around the corner from the living room at the front of their home.

"I'm just getting something to drink, Mom!" The lanky teenager put back a plastic-wrapped hunk of ham and grabbed a bottle of soda before closing the fridge and taking the stairs two at a time to his bedroom with Ivory at his heels.

"Looks like Nathan has found a new friend and I've lost a dog," Darien said.

"For now, maybe," Jack replied. "Beth and I agreed no more pets after the cat went to feline heaven."

Darien pulled out and sat down in the chair across the table from his brother. "Nothing and nobody to tie you down once Nathan goes off to college."

"That's right. I'm even thinking about early retirement so my wife and I can do all the things we've always wanted to do but haven't had the time."

Darien turned away. "Yeah, you never know how much time you've got left."

Jack winced at the pain in his brother's voice. "I'm sorry, D. That was incredibly insensitive of me."

Darien drank his coffee and changed the subject. "So. Early dinner?"

Jack put down the red pen in his hand and shoved his students' work aside. "The folks haven't seen you in a year. We've all got some catching up to do."

"Then I better get ready for the inquisition." Darien stood and headed for the guest bathroom and shower.

Donna wept in the arms of her younger son as though he had been resurrected from the dead. Stewart's strong and steady bear hug warmed Darien's heart. Hannah punched his arm in familiar greeting. Her fiancé Evan pumped his arm in a hearty handshake.

"I'm not sure if you remember me, sir," Evan said.

Darien laughed and slapped him on the back. "Of course I remember you, Evan. Congratulations on your new job and making the wise decision to marry my best girl. We're family now, so skip the formality and don't call me 'sir'."

"And don't be late for dinner, which is now being served in the dining room," Jack interrupted.

Darien relished every delicious dish served and savored words spoken and sentiments shared around the table with the family he loved and had sorely missed. His father commiserated another losing season for his Mets. His brother described the frustrations and little victories in the English Lit classroom and on the sidelines coaching his high school players to a disappointing yet satisfying second place finish on the New Jersey state ball diamonds. His mother did her best to update Darien on all the Hoboken and Montclair gossip – who had moved, changed careers, married, divorced, birthed children and welcomed grandchildren. Beth and Hannah updated everyone on wedding plan details to Evan's obvious embarrassment. Nathan said little but ate the most, devouring heaping plates of food.

"So, Darien, fill us in on your year away," Beth requested. "What's kept you in Iowa?"

Darien pushed back his empty plate and wiped his mouth with his napkin. "Well, I think you all know I bought a farmhouse and fixed it up."

"We all wondered why you did that, dear," his mother said.

"I made a ridiculously low ball offer for the place by East Coast standards and the owners accepted because it was in pretty rough shape. The renovation kept me busy for months after I finished the restaurant consulting jobs."

"Not like you needed the money from the jobs or flipping a fixer upper," Jack said.

"No, but I needed projects to focus on."

"What's the town like, son? Harmony, isn't it?" his father asked.

Darien nodded. "It's tiny, population only about 2,500. But they're good people."

"Have you made friends there?" Stewart wanted to know.

Hannah at his left poked her uncle in the ribs with her elbow. "Any we should know about?"

Nathan snorted and rolled his eyes. "What a nosy rosy."

"A few," Darien answered his father and grinned at his niece in silent reply.

"Will you be going back to Iowa, dear?" Donna asked.

"I'm not sure. I might go back for closing. Before I left, I listed the farmhouse with the real estate agent who helped me buy it."

"So you're selling the house, son?" his father asked.

Darien nodded. "Stan thinks he can get a good offer. But I promise I'll stay for the wedding and the holidays. If the house sells before then, the lawyers and agents will just have to work out the details without me."

Dishes eventually travelled from table to dishwasher and good-nights were exchanged. The McKenna elders left for their Hoboken brownstone with Stewart behind the wheel of his prized Buick sedan. Evan kissed his fiancée at the end of the driveway and walked the three blocks to his parents' house. Beth and Hannah went to their respective upstairs bedrooms and Nathan took Ivory for another long walk, leaving Darien and Jack to talk over mugs of stout local brew.

"OK, D," Jack said. "What's really going on in bum-fuck Iowa? And don't forget our 'no BS' rule."

"I didn't lie."

"But you didn't tell the whole truth."

"I did put the house up for sale and I have made friends. Buck and his wife Shayla. They own the local cafe. Sam and Miranda, Ivory's veterinarian and her sister."

"The same Miranda I asked to check on you when you had your meltdown?"

"There's only one Miranda that I know of in Harmony." Darien got up, crossed the kitchen and opened the refrigerator. "Another beer?"

Jack nodded. Darien popped tops from bottles, refilled their mugs and settled down again at the kitchen table. "So do tell the details. Why did you run off to Wisconsin?"

Darien swallowed a mouthful of beer and licked the foam from his lips, stalling for time and the truth. "Miranda was concerned about me and I was rude to her. So I invited her to dinner at the farmhouse. I pulled out all the stops, wined and dined her, made her a three course meal that I'm afraid she enjoyed a bit too much."

"How so?"

"Apparently, Miranda doesn't drink. I swear to you, Jack, I had no idea a couple glasses of wine would affect her that much."

"She got drunk."

"Well, no, not drunk. But not sober enough to drive back into town."

"So she stayed the night."

"Yeah."

"Go on."

"I'd had a glass or two while I was cooking dinner."

"And a couple more with dinner." Darien nodded. "I think I can guess what happened next."

Darien finished his beer in three long gulps. "God, Jack. She looked so good lying there stretched out on the rug and the pillows in front of the fireplace. I'd never seen her with her hair down. She's got this long red hair almost to her waist and incredible green eyes and these perfectly round, firm …"

"I get the picture."

"It had been so long and I was so lonely. I gave in and made the biggest mistake of my life."

"Did you tell her that?"

"I told her everything the next morning. I told her about Ali, how I'd run away and ended up in Iowa. That I valued our friendship but I wasn't ready for anything more."

"Ouch."

"I had to tell her the truth, Jack."

"Why do I get the feeling there's more to this story?"

"Because there is. I wanted to talk to her. But I didn't have the nerve. So I ran away again."

"To Wisconsin."

Darien nodded. "When I got back I called Stan and listed the farmhouse. Miranda came out the day before I left. I told her I'd put the house up for sale. I owed that to her. She helped me out. A lot. She worked hard refinishing the old wood cabinets and the hardwood floors and she spent more than a few hours on the business end of a paint brush. I told her I was going back east and that I wasn't coming back. That's when she told me she's pregnant."

Jack's eyebrows went up and his beer mug came down hard on the table. "She's what, now?

"Oh, you heard me, Jack."

Jack leaned back and exhaled a low whistle. "So let me get this straight. A one night stand and she's pregnant?"

"That's right."

"Well, you always did just dive right in. What are you going to do now?"

"I honestly don't know."

"You must feel something for Miranda."

"I told you. She's a good friend."

"C'mon, D. You don't get your friend pregnant."

"That just happened."

"What about her?"

"What do you mean?"

"A woman does not make love with you if she just wants to be your friend." Jack softened his voice and his expression. "What's really holding you back? Is it Ali?"

Darien looked away and swallowed hard. "I'll never love another woman the way I love Ali."

"Of course you won't. Love is different every time." Jack slung his arm across his brother's slumped shoulders. "Darien, Ali is gone. Miranda is here. And she's going to have your child, the most incredible gift a woman will ever give you."

"I don't even know if Miranda wants me in her life. She told me she needs financial support. And I accept that responsibility. I'll give her and the baby whatever they need."

"But not you." Jack patted his brother's back. "D, you know I've got your back no matter what you decide. I may not agree with it. But I'll always be there for you."

"Thanks, man."

Letting Go

Chapter 18

Darien delayed crossing the Brooklyn Bridge until he ran out of reasons to stay in New Jersey. He grinned through Hannah's graduation, took charge of Beth's kitchen at Thanksgiving, and gaped in wide-eyed wonder at the beautiful bride his niece had become. He slept in his Hoboken boyhood bedroom on Christmas Eve, stayed in pajamas like the boy of Christmas past the next morning and opened presents with his parents. He raised a glass of beer with Jack and toasted the New Year while the midnight drop of the ball in Times Square flickered on the wide screen in his brother's living room. He called the ski resort in Vermont the next morning to confirm that all of the newlywed's honeymoon expenses would be charged to his credit card.

Ivory nudged him awake with her nose the morning of the day he intended to return to the top floor apartment on Water Street. Darien stretched, rubbed his dog's ears, and reached for his cellphone.

"Hey, David, it's Darien."

"Happy New Year!"

"Same to you. I've got a load of stuff to haul in the freight elevator. Can you meet me around back in a couple hours?"

"Where are you now?"

"I've been in Jersey since before Thanksgiving. Sorry I didn't call sooner."

"Well, this is a pleasant surprise. Hey, Jayson, Darien's back," David called to his partner. "I'll let Mimi and Kenny know," he told Darien. "See you at 10." And he hung up.

"Damn it," Darien swore under his breath.

"What's wrong, D?" Jack stood barefoot and shirtless in the guest bedroom doorway toweling his hair dry.

"I wanted to ease back into Brooklyn without a lot of fanfare. But I told David the town crier and now all bets are off."

Jack sat on the bed beside his brother. "Not up to facing the inquisition?"

Darien grunted. "Something like that."

"Want me to go with you?"

Darien nodded. "Yeah, I'd like that."

Darien spotted David's waving arms and beaming smile a block away. David yanked opened the driver's side door, fist bumped the driver and shook Jack's hand.

"Good to see you again, Jack!" David bear-hugged Darien as soon as the much taller man's shoes hit pavement. "Welcome home!"

Ivory bounded from the back seat in a show of protection for her person. "It's OK, girl," Darien reassured her.

"Who's this?" David stepped back and extended his closed fist for the white dog to sniff. Her blue eyes stared into his. "Where did you find this beauty?" he asked Darien.

"I rescued her from a shelter. Her name is Ivory."

"C'mon, Ivory." David tapped his palm against his thigh. "Let's go check out your new digs."

With the Range Rover's cargo emptied and stacked in the appropriate tidy rooms, the three men made the rounds of the nearby markets. Darien loaded up on the culinary delights and delicacies he'd craved and couldn't get in Iowa. Jack sat on a stool at the island in the center of the spacious apartment's kitchen and watched David's expert hands create an appetizing antipasti platter of marinated vegetables and gourmet olives, asiago and fontina cheese and melon to wrap with prosciutto while Darien prepared pasta carbonara with crisp bacon and fresh snapped peas. Jayson arrived with a homecoming bottle of Chianti the four men enjoyed with the opulent meal.

Darien relayed the details of his time in Iowa without mentioning Miranda or the baby. Jayson boasted about his growing fashion design business and David reported no problems with the building or the tenants.

"We do have something to tell you, Darien," David said.

Darien set his wine glass on the side table and sank back into the butter softness of the leather sofa. "What's up?" he asked.

David smiled at Jayson. "We finally got married last April."

"Congratulations. But that was a given. Tell me something I wouldn't know."

Jayson reached for and squeezed his husband's hand. "It took me awhile to win him over. "But David and I have agreed we're ready to be parents."

"We contacted an adoption agency in Queens and filled out all the forms," David explained. "We'd about given up when we got the call last week."

David's smile broadened. "It was love at first sight. Our little girl is so precious. I held her in my arms and she wrapped these tiny fingers around my thumb." David sighed. "I was a goner."

"We both were," Jayson said. "We signed the papers and handed her back to the case worker." He rolled his ocean green eyes. "That wasn't easy. We wanted to take her home right then and there. We got up to go, and ..." Jayson squeezed David's hand again. "You tell the rest of the story."

"There's more?" Darien asked.

David nodded. "This little boy with big brown eyes was staring at us from the hallway. He looked a lot like the baby we'd just adopted. So we asked the case worker and she told us he was her brother."

"What could we do?" Jayson asked. "We couldn't stand the idea of separating siblings."

"So you're going to adopt them both," Darien said.

"Yes," David and Jayson said together.

"We've been looking for a house to buy and quite frankly there's nothing in Brooklyn in our price range," David said. "We're not happy about moving away. But there's no way all four of us can live here in our one bedroom apartment."

Darien rubbed his forehead. "So I guess this means I'm losing my building manager," he said.

David nodded again. "Sorry to drop this on you when you just got back," he apologized.

Jack clapped his hands together to break the long seconds of awkward silence. "Hey, life goes on, right? You're taking on a big responsibility and giving a couple of kids a home. That is commendable. Congratulations," he said and toasted their decision with his nearly empty glass of wine.

Jack refused Darien's offer to drive him to the train station in Hoboken. "You've had a long day, man. I can take the subway."

"I'll walk with you." Darien locked up the apartment and followed his brother down the steps to the street. Kenny Wong stopped them at the entrance to Clarke Media Consultants.

"Hey, Darien!" Kenny's warm smile and firm handshake drew them into the main office. Darien didn't recognize the fresh young face behind the desk Mimi had always occupied. "Sonja, this is Darien McKenna."

Sonja's dark eyelashes fluttered and her cheeks flushed. The slender hand with long nails painted red trembled when Darien clasped it. Jack smirked at the typical female reaction to his brother's extreme good looks. "I'm Jack, Darien's ugly brother," he said and nudged an elbow into Darien's ribs.

Sonja giggled.

"Where's Mimi?" Darien asked.

"Right here," she said from the doorway of the inner office.

Darien took two steps toward her and stopped. The massive mahogany desk that once belonged to Ali's corporate CEO father was gone from the executive suite where Ali once worked. A sleek modern workstation made of glass and steel had taken its place. A large framed oil portrait of Ali's likeness, so real he longed to touch it, hung on the wall behind Mimi's desk chair.

Mimi wrapped her arm around his waist and turned to look at what he admired. "Do you like it?" she asked him.

He blinked fast and swallowed hard against the lump in his throat. "Very much," he managed.

Jack tapped his brother on the shoulder. "Hey, D. I hate to break this up. But I gotta go."

"Right." Darien turned and took Mimi's small hands in his. "We'll talk more tomorrow," he said and kissed her cheek.

He walked Ivory to the East River front that evening along the same route and path he'd taken Max on so many days over too brief years. He found the bench Ali bought for them and traced the letters she'd had engraved. *From your brown-eyed girl.*

He sat on the bench and dropped his head in his hands. "Ali, my love," he whispered. "What am I going to do?"

Chapter 19

The house was so quiet Jack could hear squirrels padding across the snow-covered rooftop above his bedroom. He stretched the full length of the queen-sized bed and opened his eyes after a much-needed mid-afternoon nap. He hadn't slept through the night since he'd forced himself to let go of Hannah at LaGuardia's international terminal and made his new son-in-law promise to take care of her in the land down under. His night and day dreams were filled with memories of cradling her in his trembling hands as the doctor cut the umbilical cord, watching her pull herself up and take shaky first steps on tiny toddler bare feet, and reading her bedtime stories until her drooping eyelids closed and he tucked her under a fluffy pink Sleeping Beauty quilt.

The insistent jangling of the phone brought him back to the present.

"Hello?"

"Hey, Jack." Darien's deep voice echoed in his ear.

"Hey, D. What's up?"

"Are you? You sound half asleep."

"That's because I just woke up."

"Have you and Beth got plans tonight?"

"Beth went shopping with her friends. Last I heard, they were planning to gossip over dinner and take in a movie. So I'm on my own."

"Bring your butt to Brooklyn. There's a couple of beers here with your name on it."

"I'm on my way."

The mini-mountain of boxes on and around the dining room table was the only visible clutter in the top floor of the four-story building where Darien had loved and lived with Ali. Jack took the opened bottle of beer his brother handed him. "Got a glass or are they all going to Goodwill?"

 Darien laughed and reached into an upper cupboard. "I'm leaving a few things behind for the new owners."

Jack choked on his mouthful of brew. "You sold the building?"

"Not all of it. Mimi and Kenny still hold the lease with option to buy on the main floor offices. I totally intend to sell that space to them when they're ready. David and Jayson are buying this apartment. Jayson plans to rent the apartment they've been living in for his office and studio. David will stay on and manage the other apartments."

Jack pulled the stool away from the kitchen island and sat down hard. "Whoa! When did all this transpire?"

"Don't get too comfortable and keep your coat on. I'll tell you all about it over burgers."

"Are we going out?"

"We're going up." Darien grabbed his coat from the hook near the door that led to the fire escape.

"Are you crazy? It's January, not June."

"The grill is hot and the fire pit is on. Drink enough beer and we won't feel the cold."

"Drink enough beer and I won't make it home."

"So phone Beth and tell her you're staying here tonight to help me finish packing tomorrow."

"That will require an explanation I don't have yet," Jack muttered. He followed Darien up the fire escape to the rooftop garden spot. Their white puffs of warm breath colored the inky night cold. Nature's stars winked against the artificial lights of Brooklyn beneath and Manhattan beyond. Jack huddled at the grill next to Darien. The garlic and onion scents from sizzling meat stoked his hunger.

"Grab a plate," Darien said. Two perfect medium-well done patties came off the grill and onto buns. The brothers settled on cedar benches and all-weather cushions around the glowing fire pit.

Jack held his questions until the burgers were gone and two more beers had been poured. He cleared his plate and his throat. "So, I take it you've made a decision."

"I have." Darien stared into the dancing flame. "David put as much labor and love into this building as Ali did. She would have been pleased that he and Jayson will raise their family here." He drummed his fingers against the beer glass in his hand. "I brought back everything I took from here and left everything from Iowa behind. I thought Miranda could help herself to whatever she wanted from the farmhouse. We'd hire an attorney to draw up a child support and joint custody agreement. We'd sign it, I'd send her money and she'd let me play Dad to our son or daughter a few weeks in the summer and every other Christmas."

"But you don't like that arrangement."

Darien shook his head. "Not so much."

"What do you want, D?"

"Mom said at dinner the day after I got back that all of you wondered why I bought the farmhouse. Remember?" Jack nodded. "I said I got a great deal on the house and I needed something to do. Those were surface reasons. I know now that I actually bought that house for Miranda." Darien's eyes softened to a pale shade of misty grey. "You should have seen the look on her face at that first walk through, Jack. She didn't have the money to make an offer. But she wanted to so badly."

Jack clicked his glass of beer against the glass in his brother's hand. "Now we're getting to the truth." Darien looked puzzled. "She couldn't afford to buy the house. So unless you planned on giving it to her, were you really buying it just for Miranda?"

Darien studied his brother's face, searching for the answer he knew they shared. "I bought it for us – for Miranda and me."

Jack smiled and slapped his brother on the back. "So what are you going to do about that, D?"

"Stan the real estate man called this afternoon. He has an offer on the farmhouse and it's a good one. But I'm going to turn it down, tell him the house is off the market."

"And?"

"I've had a couple of weeks to think about that. And I realized something about myself in the process. I never saw myself as a family man. I was a chef. Maybe that's the main reason why I fell so hard for Ali. She was as focused on her career as I was. And she was older. She couldn't have children. But she wanted them. Did I tell you that?"

Jack shook his head no.

"Remember when she disappeared a few days before we got married and everyone was looking for her?"

Jack nodded. "Beth was frantic about deciding on centerpieces for the wedding reception."

Darien smiled at the memory. "I found Ali at the art museum staring at a Monet. She said she wished we'd been the same age, that we'd met in school, married young, had kids and grandkids, if that's what we wanted. I didn't care about any of that. I loved her so much." Darien finished his beer and stared into the fire pit flame. "I still can't say that I love Miranda."

"But you're going back."

Darien nodded. "I have to. I need to be there for her and the baby. I've got to find out if we can be a family." He grinned. "Besides, I'm starting to warm up to the idea of being Dad."

Jack smiled. "I knew you would." He moved closer, shoulder-to-shoulder with his brother. "Man, I'm freezing," was his excuse. They shared one last New York City night on the rooftop until snow at midnight drove them inside to soft beds and warm blankets.

The movers arrived at two the next afternoon. "Only the boxes, sir?" asked the slender uniformed man with the clipboard. "No furniture?"

Darien shook his head and looked around. He hesitated when his steel gaze landed on the only piece in the expansive living area that he'd brought with him when he'd moved in with Ali. The well-worn leather wingback chair had been a gift from Darien's long departed mentor and dear friend. He couldn't leave it behind. "Just this chair," he replied and pointed.

"Well, this is it." David stood in the apartment's open front door. A sad half-smile crossed his fine-featured face. "It doesn't seem all that long ago I was helping you move in."

"I know what you mean." Darien stood in the spot where his lips had first met Ali's, focused on the table for two at the kitchen window where they'd shared breakfast and a newspaper in the morning and a glass of wine at night, settled on the open French doors to the bedroom where they'd made love. "This was home. But I can't stay here. She's everywhere. But she's gone." He walked across the hardwood floor and put his hands on David's slumped shoulders. "This place is yours now. Yours and Jayson's and … what are their names again?"

David's smile brightened. "I don't think I've told you. Our son's name is Joshua. But he prefers Josh. We named our little girl Alicia."

Darien smiled. "I didn't tell you why I'm going back to Iowa. I met a woman there. We didn't plan for it to happen. But …"

David's pale blue eyes opened wide. "Hello papa!" He bear hugged a laughing Darien.

Ivory trotted to the road-ready Range Rover, packed and parked on Water Street. "Let's take a walk first, girl," Darien said and led her to the familiar path along the East River. He immersed himself one last time in the sights, sounds and scents – grasping, clutching, assimilating every nuance in great detail for the days, nights and years ahead without and away from the city he loved. He stopped at the bench – read, recited, memorized what Ali had written there until Ivory pulled at the leash that connected him to her and the present.

He patted her head and rubbed her ears. "You'd never be happy here, would you, girl?" She sneezed, pointed her nose at the leaden sky and uttered a deep, guttural howl in reply.

"Time to go." His eyes traced the Manhattan skyline. "Good bye, New York." He touched his gloved fingers to his lips and pressed them against the words inscribed on the bench. "Good bye, my love," he whispered.

The Promise

Chapter 20

Darien stopped at his boyhood home on his way west to tell his parents the real reason for his return to Iowa. His mother cried tears of both joy and bitter separation, happy at the impending birth of a grandchild but sad to see her son leave to begin a new life far away. Stewart comforted his wife and congratulated Darien on a decision well made.

Two long days on the road later, Darien crossed the Mississippi River and drove past the harvested corn and soybean fields on either side of Iowa's stretch of interstate. His anxiety level rose with each mile marker.

"What am I going to say to her, Ivory?" he asked. His companion's blue eyes studied him and her perked up ears swiveled as he spoke. "Hi, Miranda. I'm back," he rehearsed. "How about moving in with me? The house has enough bedrooms for you and the baby." Ivory shook her head and sneezed. "Yeah, she'd probably hit me. OK, how about this. Miranda, we'll convert the barn into your studio. You could challenge yourself as an artist, do murals or maybe get into sculpture or even concrete fountains. We could hire a nanny. What do you say?" Ivory rumbled Husky talk punctuated with a vocal yawn. "Nah, no good either." He turned on the radio to drown out the sound of his heart pounding in his ears.

"Enjoy those sunny skies and mild temperatures today, Marion," said the announcer, "there's a storm on the way tonight."

Darien grunted. "No kidding."

"Here's an oldie but a goodie from the late great John Denver going out to a sweet lady."

"Perfect," Darien groaned. He reached for the dashboard to silence the caller's request. Ivory barked. "What's up with you?" he asked. "You want to listen to this?" Ivory settled her chin on his leg and smacked her lips in doggie contentment. "Fine," he said and the song began.

Darien vaguely remembered the words and melody sung by an actor in a film he hadn't much liked. But by the time the lyrics ended and the last note of the song faded, he knew what he had to do. He pulled into a barren rest stop without services and shifted the idling car into park. He scanned the visual white noise of snow, sifted through his jumbled thoughts and tempered jagged emotions. He rubbed Ivory's ears and returned her blue-eyed stare.

"No question, this is a really fucked up situation. I don't know what I'm going to say to her or how I'm going to make this right, pretty girl. But somehow I've got to convince Miranda that our time has just begun."

By the time he crossed the Linn County line, Darien had decided not to announce his return by phone, which would most likely go to voice mail, but to take the direct route instead. He would go and see Miranda. He stopped at the farmhouse long enough to settle Ivory in after the long trip and continued on into Harmony. He parked the Range Rover in front of Sam's veterinary clinic, sucked in and let out a deep, steadying breath, and walked into the mercifully empty waiting room.

He stood in front of her seated in the usual spot behind the reception area desk. "Hello, Miranda."

Her green eyes flashed surprise before a forced veil of indifference descended. "Hello, Darien."

"How have you been?"

"Fine, thank you."

He shoved his trembling hands in his coat pockets. "I would have phoned first to let you know I was back in town. But I wasn't sure if you'd take the call."

Sam rounded the corner carrying a clipboard. "Hey, Mira, when did you order ..." Her question trailed off when she saw Darien. She stopped in her tracks and blinked at the apparent apparition.

"Hi, Sam," he said.

"Uh. Hi."

Darien turned back to Miranda. "Can we go somewhere and talk?"

She crossed her arms over her chest. "I'm working."

"Take a break." Sam ignored her sister's cold stare. "The house is close by and there's snack food in the fridge if you're hungry."

"Fine." Miranda stood and smoothed her sweater over her pregnancy. Darien tried not to focus on the obvious change in her body. He held her coat and the door for her. They walked to the McCullough family home in silence. Miranda turned the key in the front door and let them in.

"Can I get you anything?" she asked.

"No, thank you." He nodded toward the sofa. She sat in a chair. He sighed and sat across from her with the coffee table between them. The clock on the mantle over the fireplace ticked loud seconds into long minutes.

"There was an offer on the farmhouse. But I took it off the market," he said.

"Why was that?" she asked in a clipped, even tone.

"I've decided to come back and move in."

"How long do you plan to stay this time?" Her expressionless eyes were harder than the emeralds they resembled.

"I sold the apartment in Brooklyn."

"For a good price, no doubt."

He rubbed the back of his neck. "Actually, I practically gave it away to a good friend."

"How generous of you."

"Look, Miranda, I didn't come back here to spar with you."

"Then why did you come back?" she snapped.

Because I want to be with you! The urgency of his unspoken thought startled him. "I need to know that you're OK."

She laced her fingers over the child within. "You didn't have to move back to find out."

"Apparently I did since you wouldn't talk to me any other way."

The ring of Darien's cellphone in his coat pocket interrupted more silent minutes marked by the mantle clock's tick. "Yes?" he answered. "Tomorrow? No problem. I'll be there." He shoved the phone back into its hiding place. "The movers will be at the farmhouse tomorrow afternoon." He tried to dampen the plea in his voice and erase the desperation from his eyes. He knew he failed at both. "Can you be there to help me unpack?"

She wanted to shout *Are you serious?* She wanted to tell him to go to hell.

"What time?" she said instead.

Chapter 21

Miranda fluffed the sham-covered pillows on the master bedroom's king sized bed and smoothed the last crease from the deep burgundy quilt over snow white sheets. She crossed the wide planks of the refinished hardwood to close the window and stop the filmy white curtains held by gold rope tie backs from fluttering in a sliver of early spring breeze.

She looked away from the barren apple orchard in the backyard to the honey-tinged white tone paint she'd chosen for the walls. Along the wall were the massive mahogany armoire and multi-drawer dresser Darien bid on at an estate sale in Cedar Rapids. She'd discovered the elegant cherry wood bedside tables buried under boxes in a Harmony neighbor's attic. She marveled at the burgundy and gold wool runner area rug she and Darien had found in an Iowa City antique store on a cold day in February and chuckled at the memory of a scene outside her favorite shop in the university town.

Earl Manning, the store's owner, had waved to her through the full length glass windows. She'd smiled and waved back.

"Frequent customer?" Darien had asked her and she'd blushed. "Yes and no," she'd answered. "Earl sells unusual pieces that I'll never be able to afford."

He'd insisted they go in and browse. She'd politely inquired about the health of Earl's ailing mother and the current whereabouts of his archeologist brother. He'd shown her a selection of handmade sterling silver baubles adorned with rich onyx and fiery garnet stones he'd recently acquired. Earl lifted the delicate gold band with the perfect tear drop ruby and three clustered diamonds from its white satin perch under glass. She slipped it on her right ring finger as she'd done six visits before and sighed when she handed it back to him for someone else to admire and buy.

For nearly a month, Darien had let her choose the colors and décor for every room of the house and encouraged her to hang her favorite artwork on its walls. Only two empty upstairs bedrooms and a third half filled with unopened boxes shipped from Brooklyn and Hoboken needed purpose and arranged possessions to be useful. She'd only had to work a sturdy old wingback chair into the design of his combined home office and custom theater separated for privacy from the front room by massive pocket doors.

"I feel good when I sit in it," he'd explained.

"I can see why," she'd said. "It's a unique piece. I like it." Her approval surprised and pleased him. He surprised her when he kissed her cheek.

"Penny for them." Darien leaned against the bedroom door frame, his arms crossed over his chest, his lips and eyes smiling at her.

She shook off the tug at her heart felt whenever she looked at him and took a deep breath. "Darien, I think it's about time you told me what's really going on here," she said.

He shook his head. "I don't follow."

"Since you got back from New York and told me you weren't selling the farmhouse, we've filled up almost all the rooms with furniture and window treatments and rugs and just about anything else I chose. And I want to know why."

He shrugged. "I admire your eye for design and respect your opinion."

"No, it's more than that. You let me decorate this house as if it were my own, as though I were going to live here."

He straightened and gestured with his head toward the hallway. "I still need your help with the rest of the bedrooms."

"Are you kidding me?" She could feel her cheeks getting hot.

His laugh fueled her rising anger. "Humor me," he said, and disappeared around the corner. She muttered under her breath but followed him to the first empty room.

He flipped the wall switch inside the doorway and stood in the glow of overhead bulbs muted by a frosted glass fixture and fading afternoon sun streaming through the bare window above the front porch. "This should be the baby's room," he said and glanced at her over his shoulder. "What do you think?"

Her mouth dropped open. "What do you know about taking care of a baby?" she sputtered.

"Very little," he admitted. Darien motioned for her to follow him past the bathroom with pale grey walls, white pedestal sink, custom-made silver claw-footed tub and separate shower for two accessorized by Miranda's touches of plum and lavender.

Miranda stopped at the end of the hall and stood between Darien and two open doors to rooms on either side. "So which one will the nanny sleep in?"

"Neither. I have something else in mind." He stood so close she could feel the heat from him. "Do you remember the first time we walked through this house?" She nodded. "You were trying to decide which of these rooms would work best for your studio."

Her eyes narrowed and her jaw set. "I have a studio."

"I know you do. And I'm not suggesting you give up that space."

"Then what are you suggesting?"

He cupped her cheek in his palm and brushed her lips with his thumb. "Live here with me. Decorate our baby's nursery. Choose a room for your home studio. The other will be a guest room for now. Unless or until we have another child."

Miranda stepped back, her wide eyes swimming with tears that her shaking hands brushed away. "I don't know what to say."

"Say that you'll marry me."

She gasped and stared into the soft silver grey of his eyes, unsure of the motive or sincerity behind his words. She hugged her swollen belly. "I love you, Darien, and I want to marry you. I want to raise our child together. But I won't marry you if you're only asking me because you feel obligated to do the right thing. I have to know that you love me. I won't accept anything less."

He curled his fingers under her chin and tilted her head until their lips were nearly together. "Miranda, I do love you. I love that you tackle life head on. I love that you make me feel there's nothing we can't do together. I love that you love me." She felt the child inside her move with the gentle press of his lips on hers. "I want you to be my wife."

She turned her head, rested her cheek against his chest and looked out the window at the end of the hallway. The setting sun blazed a brilliant line on the horizon and the barn below cast long shadows across strips of melting late winter snow.

The ethereal beauty of her crowned by a halo of glowing copper red hair melted all that remained of the ice fortress around his heart and dissolved all doubt that remained.

He loved her.

"You know, it's a shame the barn is empty," she said. "I've always wanted a horse." She looked up at him and circled his waist with her arms. The sparkle in her eyes and impish smile suggested mischief. "Tell you what. You buy me a horse and I will seriously consider your proposal."

Darien's laughter echoed in the empty rooms. "Is this a non-negotiable contract?"

She nodded and smiled. "Consider it my dowry."

"Very well, Miss McCullough, I accept your terms."

"So do I, Mr. McKenna." A long delayed tender embrace and loving kiss shared at last sealed their promise. "Let's go tell Sam," she whispered.

Chapter 22

The lights were still on in the veterinary clinic at half past five and the unlocked door opened with ease. "Sam?" she called.

"Back here!" The overhead fluorescent fixture in the exam room dimmed and darkened.

"Harmony may be small," Darien scolded her, "but you really should keep the front door locked when you're here alone."

"Oh!" The sound of his voice slowed Sam's mid-spin momentum through her familiar end-of-day routine. Her coat fell from her hand and her mouth dropped open at the unfamiliar sight of Darien's arm around her sister's shoulders and hers around his waist. Both were grinning ear-to-ear. "Are you going to let me in on the joke?"

"No joke," Darien said to Sam and kissed his beaming bride-to-be.

"We're getting married!" Miranda announced.

Sam screamed, jumped and pumped her fists in the air. "Yes!" she hissed and wrapped her arms around them both.

Darien laughed. "I take it you approve."

"Of course I approve! When did this happen? Oh, who cares! It's happening! This is so great! Are you happy, Mira? Of course you're happy! I'm happy for you! All three of you!" Sam scooped up her crumpled coat and ended her high-spirited dance around the reception area at the clinic's front door. "Are you hungry? I'm hungry! Let's go celebrate!"

Smiles and nods of greeting from the dinner crowd ceased when Darien followed the McCullough sisters into Hank's Longhorn Cafe. Low grumbles and hums of semi-audible conversations swirled between the tables and stools.

"What'll it be, ladies?" Shayla handed menus to Miranda and Sam and tossed a third on the table. She tapped her pencil on the order pad and glared at Darien.

"We'll all have the special," Sam said. Shayla took back the menus and returned with two glasses of ice water on her tray.

"I'd like a glass of water too, please," Darien requested. Shayla grunted and grabbed a glass of melted ice from the next table.

"OK, I'm putting a stop to this right now." The legs on Sam's chair scraped the dining room's pitted hardwood floor. She stood up, grabbed her spoon and rapped it against the water glass. "Everybody listen up!" she shouted for attention over the diner's din. "It gives me great pleasure to announce the engagement and impending marriage of my sister Miranda to Darien McKenna."

The icy atmosphere instantly warmed and bubbled with delighted cries of 'Congratulations,' 'When's the wedding' and a raspy 'It's about time' from an elderly patron perched on a stool at the counter.

Two hours, three pieces of rhubarb pie on-the-house and countless well wishes and pats on the back later, Darien and Miranda walked Sam to her front porch. Miranda took his hand and led him down the street and around the corner to her studio. She turned the key in the lock before he could kiss her goodnight, pushed open the door and turned on the track lighting that illuminated her workspace and gallery. "Let me grab a few things before we go."

Darien closed the studio's door behind him. "Go where?"

"Back to the farmhouse." She led the way to her apartment. He stopped at the entry to her living space as if he'd stepped in super glue.

"C'mon in," she said. "I won't be long."

He coughed, curious at his own embarrassment, and watched her move around her one room kitchenette and bedroom with the sagging two-cushion couch and mini-screen TV.

"Have a seat," she said, and cleared a pile of sketchbooks from the lone chair at a 70s-era chipped and yellow speckled Formica-topped kitchen table. She frowned at him when he didn't move. "What's wrong?"

"You're going home with me tonight?"

"In case you'd forgotten, my truck is at the farmhouse."
She plopped her unzipped candy apple red travel bag on her
twin bed and filled it to side-splitting capacity. "And my
bed is not big enough for both of us."

They cuddled on the sofa, sipped steaming cups of
chamomile tea, and gazed at the hypnotic dip and leap
of flames dancing in the fireplace. Miranda patted the
upholstered cushions. "This is much more comfortable
than the floor," she said and sank deeper into his arms.

He kissed her hair and held her close. "We'll go to city hall
tomorrow and get a marriage license. We can get married
as soon as Sam has the time off. I'll ask Buck to be my
best man."

"What's the rush?"

"You're pregnant."

"That's obvious."

"Shouldn't we get married before the baby is born?"

"We haven't been too concerned about what we should do so far. Besides, I want to get married in the same size dress I wore on the night we conceived this child. And I want a wedding. Have the ceremony in the apple orchard, grill burgers, tap a keg and blast Springsteen through the home theater."

The New Jersey native chuckled at the mention of his home state's favorite rock star son. "Whatever you want, sweetheart."

Ivory nudged his hand with her perpetually wet nose. "Is that your idea of a good time too, pretty girl?" Miranda asked and scratched behind her erect ears.

"We usually take a walk around the grounds at night," Darien explained.

"Good timing. I'll go up and get ready for bed."

Darien and his dog circled the barn and patrolled the orchard on schedule. Darien waited until the bathroom window's frosted glass went dark before he whistled for Ivory. Once inside, the white dog seemed to sense her place in bed beside Darien would be occupied and settled for sleep in her fleece-lined bed beside the fireplace.

The bedroom door was closed when Darien got to the top of the stairs. He used the bathroom, brushed his teeth, discarded his clothes in the hamper and wrapped himself in the robe he kept within reach of the shower. His hand froze when he reached to turn the knob on his bedroom door.

"This is ridiculous," he muttered to himself and pushed the door open.

Miranda lay on her back. The glow from the lamp on the table at her side cast shadows that exaggerated the covered silhouette of a body not entirely her own. "Pajamas not allowed," she said, rolled on her side and threw back the blanket to reveal her nakedness. She rested her head on the plumped pile of pillows and patted the mattress with her hand.

The sheer feminine beauty of her reminded him of works of art he'd admired in paintings on museum walls. "Oh, Miranda." He went to her, entranced by the changing curve of her, the glowing vitality of her. The perfection of the firm breasts he remembered had softened to nurture new life. He reached out and touched what their joining had created.

"Are you sure we should do this? I mean, is it safe for, you know ..."

"Darien, I love you, my hormones are raging and I desperately want to make love with you."

"I've never made love with a pregnant woman before."

"And I've never been pregnant before." Her fingers opened his robe and her arms pulled him to her. "Life is full of firsts."

"So it is," he agreed. They began anew and in love with soft kisses and gentle caresses.   Mindful of her needs, changed and changing body, he let her guide the positions and rhythm of their lovemaking. She moaned with his every touch and sighed when he entered her. In afterglow, she nestled against him.

"Mmmm, Darien, that was sweet."

"Yes, it was." He held her, kissed her, felt her relax against him and surrender to sleep. "And it will be," he whispered. Images of moments past and anticipated swirled behind his closed eyes. Waves of emotion crested and fell at each breath he took with hers. He released the pain of loss, let go of guilt and welcomed the contentment of being beside her. He dismissed the fear and embraced the joy of raising a child with her. He was at peace with the place he had found for himself. For the first time in what seemed an eternity of hurt, he was happy. He sank back on the pillows and smiled into the darkness.

"Thank you, Miranda," he whispered, and slept.

Chapter 23

He felt her looking at him before he opened his eyes.
Miranda's mass of red hair covered her breasts and rained
over his chest. Her green eyes shone in the early morning
light and her fair skin contrasted rose petal pink against
the winter white linens. "You are so beautiful," he said
and raised his body and lips to hers. Her arms circled him
and they lay back together, snuggling for warmth under the
foamy down comforter.

"So where's my ring?" she asked him.

He nuzzled her neck. "You want a horse AND a ring?"

"One is my dowry. The other is required."

He laughed. "Or we're not officially engaged?"

"Oh, we're officially engaged all right. I said yes."

"Which is why you don't have a ring."

She frowned. "Explain, please."

"Well, I wasn't sure when to ask or what your answer
would be." He swung his legs over the side of their bed
and reached for his robe. "Tell you what. I'll make
breakfast and then we'll go wherever you want and pick out
your ring."

"Shower first," she said, grabbed her robe and disappeared
down the hallway. He waited until he heard the water
running to retrieve what he'd hoped to give her and hide it
where he knew she would find it.

French toast coated in egg whites, vanilla and cinnamon sizzled in the fry pan Darien tended. He felt Miranda's arms go around him and an odd ripple of movement at his back.

"That smells incredible," she said. He felt the ripple again.

He flipped the golden brown side up and turned off the stove. "Be careful near a lit burner, sweetheart."

She laughed and backed away. "That wasn't me." She took the spatula from his hand and pressed his palm to the bump beneath her loose-fit cotton shirt. The ripple kicked him.

"Oh my God!" He pulled his hand away and his eyes went wide. "Does that hurt?"

Miranda laughed at his reaction. "No. It scared me at first. But I'm getting used to it."

"You should sit down." He pulled out a chair from the kitchen table.

"Nonsense," she said. She reached into the cupboard for a pair of plates and began to set the table. She opened the utensil drawer. "What's this?" Her fingers closed around a small white box nestled between the forks and spoons.

Darien grinned. "You won't know unless you open it."

The hinge on the box clicked. Miranda gasped at the custom-crafted artisan's ring with a trio of diamonds surrounding the perfect tear drop ruby set in a spiral of shimmering gold. Darien plucked the ring from the box and slipped the band on the third finger of her left hand.

"I went back for it the next day. I would have given it to you even if you'd said no."

Her arms circled his neck and he felt her warm tears on his chest. "I love you so much," she whispered.

He stroked her hair and held her close. "I love you." His heart beat with hers.

Chapter 24

Jack nibbled on the tuna salad sandwich Beth had made for him and sipped iced tea from his glass. She sat across from him at their kitchen table with her own sandwich and drink. But she wasn't eating.

He looked up. "What's up?" he asked.

"I was going to ask you the same question."

"Any particular topic?"

"Why you're encouraging Nathan to go to the University of Iowa."

Jack shrugged. "Our son wants to be a writer. He can't do any better than the Iowa Writer's Workshop."

"I don't agree. Our alma mater's English program ranks in the top 10."

"Beth, he doesn't want to go to Columbia."

"What about New York University? Professors there have won Pulitzer prizes." She leaned toward him to make her point. "He could stay here at home with us."

Jack finished his sandwich and licked his fingers. "He needs to find his own way away from us."

Her eyes narrowed above her frown. "You want an excuse to visit the campus and meet the woman who lured Darien to Iowa."

Jack started to protest. But he couldn't compose an argument. Beth knew him too well. And she was right.

"OK, so what if I do. What's wrong with that?"

"Nothing, as long as you agree that where Nathan goes to college is up to him."

He reached across the table they'd shared in the only home they'd lived in since the day he'd married and carried her through the front door. In 20 years, they'd filled the once-empty rooms with love and family. He took her hand, leaned over their lunch, and kissed her as he had when he'd promised her a lifetime. "I do," he said.

Two weeks later, Jack and Nathan boarded a jumbo jet in Newark bound for a three hour flight and equally long layover at Chicago O'Hare prior to take off in a much smaller plane headed to Cedar Rapids.

Father and son shifted and squirmed to obtain illusive comfort on the final leg of their westward journey. Bags of pretzels and a rubbery chicken sandwich left a bad taste in Jack's mouth and a big hole in his stomach. His mouth watered for anything prepared by Chef Darien.

The cabin speakers crackled to life. "We're on our final approach into Cedar Rapids. Please make sure your tray table is in the upright position and stow any personal items under the seat in front of you."

"Hallelujah," Jack muttered.

Nathan's nose was pressed against the egg-shaped window. "Wow! There's nothing but fields for miles."

Jack searched the landscape for signs of modern civilization. "Do you see the airport?" he asked his son seconds before the wheels beneath them engaged concrete. Nathan unsnapped his seat belt when the plane stopped moving, grabbed his backpack and vaulted over his father. Jack swore under his breath and trailed his lanky offspring into the terminal.

"Hey, Uncle D!" Nathan shouted and bounded into Darien's outstretched arms.

"How's my guy?" Darien laughed and hugged his nephew. "Where's your Dad?"

"Right here dragging his rear." Jack struggled with his own carryon and the suitcase Nathan had abandoned in his dash from the plane. "Thanks for the help, pal," he scolded his son.

"Here, I'll take that," Darien offered and relieved his brother of the burden. "You two grab what's on the carousel."

"Where's the shuttle to the parking lot?" asked Jack.

"There's no shuttle. We walk to the car." Jack rolled tired eyes and Darien laughed again. "No worries, man. Everything is close by in Iowa."

Nathan chattered about his plans for college and scheduled university campus tour the next day during the half hour drive to Harmony. Jack yawned, closed his eyes and heard his stomach grumble.

Darien heard it, too. "Hungry?" he asked.

"Starving," his brother replied.

"The steaks are seasoned and ready for the grill. Miranda made potato salad and a lemon meringue pie."

"She cooks, too?" Nathan asked.

"Yep, and she's pretty good at it," Darien bragged.

The Range Rover rounded the final curve and pulled into the driveway. Ivory ran from behind the farmhouse and straight to Nathan.

"Hey, girl! You remembered me!" Nathan dropped and rolled with the happy Husky in the lush green lawn of early May.

Jack closed the passenger side door and low whistled. "Big and rustic!" he said to Darien. "How much house and land do you own?"

"Twenty four hundred square feet and a barn on fourteen acres," Darien replied.

"I have got to send pictures to Mom!" Nathan snapped and downloaded digital images from his smart phone all the way up and on to the front porch.

"Could I get some help with the luggage, please?" Jack pleaded as the front screen door slammed behind Nathan and the white dog's curled up tail. Jack shook his head and cursed out loud. "I don't know what's gotten into that kid."

Darien laughed and pulled suitcases from the back of the Range Rover. "He's seventeen." The brothers transferred the load to the front entryway of the farmhouse. Jack knelt on the hardwood floor and rummaged through the soft-sided black bag that had made the trip in the belly of planes.

"What are you looking for?" Darien asked.

"Beth packed something to give Miranda." He dug deep and retrieved a V-shaped pillow. "She said it's helped ease the aches of every pregnant woman she's known, herself included."

"How thoughtful of her."

Jack looked up and into the greenest eyes he'd ever seen on the top side of a pronounced baby bump. He handed up the pillow and stood to meet the mother of his brother's child. She was everything Darien had described and more, much taller than he imagined with a soothing voice and genuine smile.

Darien wrapped a protective arm around her. "Jack, this is Miranda."

"Pleased to meet you," Jack took the hand she offered in both of his.

"It's always nice to put a face to a voice," she said.

"Dad! Come check out Uncle D's awesome man cave!" Nathan called out from behind the partially open pocket doors that divided the large main living area.

Jack cringed. "I apologize for my son's missing manners," he said. "Later, Nathan. Come in here and say hi to Miranda."

Jack and Nathan devoured steaks grilled to order and ate heaping helpings of Miranda's potato salad. Jack praised her baking skills with words while his son did the same by holding his plate up and asking for a third piece. Miranda excused herself and climbed the stairs clutching her pregnancy pillow. Darien took his guests on a quick tour of the farmhouse that ended at the upstairs guest room. An exhausted Jack flopped on the queen-sized guest bed and told his son to choose a side.

"Uncle D, is it OK if I sleep downstairs?"

Jack pretended to pout. "What, you don't want to share a bed with me?"

Nathan gave an honest answer. "Sorry, Dad. You snore."

Darien laughed. "He's right. You can saw the logs, Jack. The couch doesn't pull out but it is pretty comfortable."

Nathan tucked a pillow from the bed under each arm and eyed the down comforter. "Do you have some spare blankets? I'd really like to sleep on the back porch."

Darien grinned at his nephew. "Let's go see what we can find in the closets," he said.

Jack awoke alone in unfamiliar darkness. He threw off the sheet and comforter covering him and was immediately cooled by a whisper of breeze through an open window. The fog in his brain parted. *Iowa. Darien's farmhouse.* He reached across the unoccupied side of the mattress. *Where's Nathan?*

He got up and stubbed his toe on the suitcase that someone, probably Darien, brought up and set on the floor at the foot of the bed. He dug out slippers, a robe and the travel penlight Beth insisted he pack. The mini LED lit a precise path down the hallway, past the master bedroom's closed door, and down the flight of stairs. He paced the empty rooms, circled back to the kitchen and out onto the screened-in back porch.

His son lay in a swirl of blankets, pillows and a white dog. Jack smiled, turned and started back to bed.

"Dad?" Nathan whispered.

"Yes, son."

"Go outside and look up at the sky. There's so many more stars in Iowa."

Chapter 25

Jack followed the Range Rover's GPS instructions for an uneventful drive to and from the University of Iowa. Darien declined the invitation to join them and handed over the keys, preferring to stay home and close to Miranda.

Jack finished the tour impressed with the faculty, curriculum and philosophy of the program. He left campus convinced from Nathan's wide-eyed reactions and enthusiastic responses that his son would leave the East Coast for Iowa City at the end of his upcoming senior year in high school.

Nathan's excitement led his uncle to the same conclusion. "Looks like another McKenna is moving to Iowa," Darien observed. The brothers finished a beer and opened a second while the teenager's ginger beer sat untouched on the kitchen table they'd gathered around.

Jack changed the subject when Nathan stopped talking and drank his alcohol-free brew. "When is Miranda due?" he asked Darien.

"End of the month," Darien answered.

"She's no doubt pretty uncomfortable."

"Yeah, she gets tired easily. She sleeps but not for long."

Jack chuckled. "I remember those days. And nights."

Nathan swallowed the last of his ginger beer and burped. "She's really big. Hey! Will Hannah get big like that when she has a baby? That would be so awesome. She'd really hate that."

A stifled sob from the staircase interrupted Jack's stern response. Miranda stood on the bottom step with one hand over her mouth, the other on the bump beneath her breasts.

"Miranda, honey," Darien said. "Did we wake you?"

Tears flowed and the sobs followed. Miranda turned and waddled back up the stairs.

"Oh, geez," Darien said and gulped the rest of his beer.

"I don't envy you that scene, bro," Jack said.

"Thanks for the encouraging words," he muttered and followed her.

Jack shot a sideways glance at his son and rolled his eyes.

"What did I say?" Nathan asked.

Jack drank the last of his beer. "My son, you've got a lot to learn about women."

Darien sat beside Miranda on the bed and held her hand until she stopped crying. She wiped her face and blew her nose in tissues from the box she kept on her side table.

205

"Feel any better?" he asked.

"No. Now I've got a headache and I can't take any aspirin because I'm pregnant and I feel like I've been pregnant forever and I'll be pregnant the rest of my life."

He grinned. "I hope not." She frowned at him. "Sweetheart, in a few weeks, the baby will be here and you'll be so busy being a new mom you won't even remember being pregnant."

"That's easy for you to say," she snapped. "Your body is still yours. I'm sharing mine. And I'm tired of being fat!"

"You're not fat, Miranda."

"Then what am I?"

He brushed loose strands of damp copper hair away from her face and kissed her flushed cheek. "You're beautiful."

"Oh, Darien, look at me! My hands are so swollen I can't wear my engagement ring. My belly is so big I haven't seen my shoes in weeks and my feet feel like a pair of inflated balloons."

Darien stood, plumped and stacked all their bed's pillows against the headboard behind her, and handed her the V-pillow that cradled her baby. "Lay back and get comfortable, love," he said.

"As comfortable as I CAN get," she said and settled against the pillows. He lifted her legs onto the comforter, sat back on the bed and put her feet in his lap. He rubbed her aching ankles and arches. She moaned in relief.

"I don't know what else I can do," he began.

"This is a good start," she assured him.

"Or what else I can say except I love you."

"Why?"

He looked at her, puzzled. "Excuse me?"

"Why do you love me?"

He went on rubbing her feet. "Because you didn't say no."

Now she looked puzzled and her eyes narrowed. "When?"

"When I asked you to marry me. You could have taken the money and legally limited the time I'd have with our child. You could have shut me out and not given us a chance to be a family. But you said yes. You let me in to your life. I love you because we are going through this together and we have so much more love and life ahead of us." He reached for, held and caressed her fingers. "I love you because you will be my wife and there's no one else I'd rather spend the rest of my life with than the mother of my child and the woman I love."

She started to cry again. But these tears streamed around the turned up corners of a wide smile. "Oh, Darien," she said. "You really do love me."

He took her left hand in his and slid an invisible band on her ring finger. "Yes, I do," he said.

New Life

Chapter 26

Summer spread a stifling blanket of heat over the Midwest a month before the official start of the season on the calendar. Afternoons of pop-up showers raised the relative humidity to a shirt-soaking steam and the lawn to ankle-topping height almost every morning. Darien cursed the weather and pushed the mower around acres of lawn that seemed to stretch for miles.

"Howdy, neighbor!" Stan the real estate man got out of the sedan he'd parked in the farmhouse driveway. He waved at Darien blazing the trail of newly-cut grass. A younger man Darien did not recognize got out of the passenger's side door. Darien silenced the mower's sputtering engine and wiped ribbons of sweat from his eyes with the side towel stuffed in his work pants pocket. "We're on our way into town to close on the McMurty place. This is Trevor Grady, the new kid on the block. Trevor, meet my former client, Darien McKenna, the owner of this property."

Darien wiped his hands and shook the hand offered in greeting. "Trevor got transferred by his employer to Cedar Rapids from Portland, Oregon," Stan explained.

"Bringing family along?" Darien asked.

Trevor smiled. "Just Macduff, my sheepdog."

Darien smiled back. "Then you're as crazy as I was when I bought this place."

"That's why I brought Trevor out here to meet you. The McMurty place isn't as big or run down as this old girl was when you signed on the dotted line. But it is a fixer-upper."

"I'm up for the challenge." Trevor brushed flies and damp blonde bangs from his forehead.

"Have you got time to go inside for a cold drink and a quick tour?" Darien offered.

Stan looked at his watch. "We've got a half hour or so to spare."

Darien and the real estate agent described the pre-renovation condition of the farmhouse. Trevor admired the restored front porch and asked questions laced with compliments during the tour.

"I'd take you upstairs, but my fiancée is resting," Darien explained.

"How soon is that baby due?" Stan asked.

"Any day now," Darien said. He pulled out chairs at the kitchen table for his guests and opened a kitchen cupboard door. "Beer or iced tea?"

Trevor grinned. "I'd love a beer, but I'll pass to keep a clear head."

"I'm driving," said Stan.

Darien set drink glasses and a pitcher of iced tea from the fridge on the table. "And I'm still mowing."

"After we finish up at the office, I'm taking Trevor over to the farm implement dealer in Marion to order up the proper equipment for handling acres of grass," Stan said. "Would you like to come along?"

"Man, that is a great idea," Darien said. "But I can't leave Miranda."

As if on cue, Sam opened and stepped through the front door carrying a bag of groceries. "Hey, Darien, I thought I'd drop off a few essentials." Her usual frenetic forward motion abruptly halted when she saw Trevor.

He sprang from his chair without introduction or hesitation. "Let me help you," he said and took the groceries from her. They stood inches apart, a paper shopping bag between them, silent and staring into the other's eyes.

Darien and Stan observed the obvious and exchanged raised eyebrow and half-smile reactions.

"Thanks," said Sam.

"My pleasure," Trevor answered without taking his blue eyes off hers.

Darien got up and took the bag from Trevor. "You'll want to get to know Sam. She's Harmony's only veterinarian and, in my biased opinion, the best in the county."

"You live here?" Sam asked Trevor.

"He's buying the McMurty place and we need to get going," Stan reminded his client.

"I have a dog, a sheepdog," Trevor told her.

Stan tapped Trevor on the shoulder. "Time to sign 30 years of your life away and then it's off to Marion, my friend."

"Right." Darien snapped his fingers in front of Sam's nose to get her attention. "Can you stay with Miranda while I go with Stan and Trevor and buy a bigger mower?"

Sam blinked. "Sure."

"We'll pick you up in about an hour," Stan said.

"Perfect. That'll give me time to finish the front and get cleaned up." Darien opened the front door for his guests and crossed the porch and half-cut lawn to the mower he'd abandoned near Stan's car.

"Have you set a wedding date yet?" Stan asked Darien.

"End of July here at the house. You're both invited."

Trevor's glazed over glance looked back at the farmhouse front door. "Will she be at the wedding?"

Darien and Stan grinned at each other. "Sam is the maid of honor," Darien replied.

Darien returned home with an invoice that promised his new toy would be delivered the next day. He turned his good mood and charm on the older woman seated across from Sam at the kitchen table.

"Who are you, lovely lady," he said.

"Hello, Daddy Darien." Her black-as-coal eyes glistened under a thick cloud of salt-and-pepper hair. The canary-yellow smock she wore overlapped arms that sagged with age. Baggy cornflower blue pants covered white clogs on her small feet.

Sam rolled her eyes. "Darien, you met Cherise at Doctor Gregson's office."

"Oh, yes," he said. "My apologies."

"None needed," she said. "You and Miranda are about to experience a major life-changing event. It stands to reason you'll forget a few minor details."

"So you're Doctor Gregson's nurse."

Sam rolled her eyes again. "Cherise is Miranda's midwife. She's going to deliver the baby."

Darien looked puzzled. "So you'll assist the doctor at the hospital? In the delivery room?"

The women looked at each other. "I'll deliver the baby here," Cherise clarified.

Darien felt his level of surprise intensify to apprehension. "By here you mean *here*? *At the house*?"

Cherise nodded. "Yes. This was discussed at Miranda's last visit."

"It was?"

"You were there, Darien. So was I," Sam reminded him. "It's what Miranda wants."

Darien's full-blown panic shifted from Sam to the midwife. "Will you excuse me?" he said and took the stairs two-at-a-time to the second floor master bedroom. Miranda was sitting propped up in bed against pillows, flipping pages in a magazine.

"Sweetheart, where are you going to have the baby?"

She closed the magazine and looked at him, puzzled. "Well, here, of course. That's what we agreed on."

He shook his head. "No, we didn't."

She nodded. "Yes, we did. We talked with Cherise a couple weeks ago."

214

Darien rubbed his jaw and paced the floor. "Miranda, I don't think this is a good idea."

"What! Why not?"

He stopped pacing and stood next to the bed. "Babies are born in a hospital. What if something goes wrong?"

She reached for and took his hand. "Babies were born at home before there were hospitals. And nothing is going to go wrong. Besides, Cherise will have help. Sam will be here."

"With all due respect, Sam is a veterinarian. You aren't having puppies!"

"Sam is a doctor and we're only having one baby, not a litter!" Her agitated expression changed abruptly to surprise. "Oh! OH! MY! MY!"

"Your what, sweetheart?"

"MY WATER BROKE!"

Darien ran down the stairs and grabbed Sam's arm. "WHERE'S THE MIDWIFE?" he shouted.

"She just left," she said and pulled her arm away. "What's wrong with you?"

"MIRANDA! BABY!" Darien ran out the front door, down the driveway and onto the highway, shouting and waving at the vehicle at the stop sign with the flashing left turn signal.

The birthing process began oddly serene. Cherise coached Miranda through physical and mental relaxation exercises and breathed with her when the pains came. The midwife filled the claw-footed tub with warm water to calm and soothe Miranda. But the contractions stopped and would not commence again until Miranda got out of the bath.

The women encouraged an anxious Darien to take breaks for his sake and theirs. He patrolled the outside perimeter of the house with Ivory until she had sniffed and marked the grass around every shrub and tree.

Eighteen hours after her first contraction, an exhausted Miranda was screaming at her baby to come out and cursing Darien for getting her pregnant. "I will NEVER let you touch me AGAIN!" she howled.

"I know you don't mean that, sweetheart," he said in the most soothing voice he could manage.

Her green eyes flashed inside dark circle orbs. "OH, YES I DO!" she screamed and clamped a five finger vice grip on Darien's forearm.

Cherise patted Darien's shoulder. "I've delivered lots of babies. Every woman says that at this stage." The midwife squatted at the foot of the bed between Miranda's bent knees. "The baby is crowning. Breathe Miranda – one, two, three – and PUSH!"

The labored sounds Miranda bellowed were more torturous than any Darien had ever heard, even worse than the screams from a line cook when he'd burned his arm with scorching deep fryer oil. He moaned with her and tears stung his bloodshot eyes.

"It's almost over, Mira," Sam crooned.

"Breathe and on the count of three," the midwife repeated.

"I CAN'T!" Miranda cried out.

"YES YOU CAN!" Cherise commanded. "One-two-three and PUSH! MIRANDA! PUSH NOW!"

Darien grimaced, closed his eyes and held his breath. The baby's cry and Miranda's audible, ragged sighs of release and relief lifted the weight from his chest. He opened his eyes.

"Oh my God, Mira, she's gorgeous!" Sam held the baby girl up for her sister to see. Cherise tended to mother and child, wrapped the squalling newborn in a thin white blanket and lay her in Miranda's arms.

"Hello, hello," Miranda whispered over and again to her daughter. Her green eyes glistened with tears.

"She looks so fragile." Darien struggled to control his trembling hands and shaky voice. "Should I touch her?"

Miranda grinned up at him. "She's yours, too."

Gently, he smoothed wisps of black hair on her tiny head and kissed the tip of her miniscule nose. He crooked his pinky finger in the palm of her hand and lost his heart at the feather light pressure of her curled fingers. Her long lashes fluttered open. Blue speckled with the unmistakable grey of his own eyes looked back at him.

Cherise leaned over the new parents and clucked her tongue. "Papa, you sure put your brand on her," she said. "Do you have a name?"

Miranda cuddled her baby against her breast, encouraging the newborn to nurse. "Marisa," she said.

Sam sighed. "That's beautiful."

Cherise agreed. "It suits her." She smiled at Darien. "Is it a family name?"

He shook his head. "First time I've heard it. But if that's what Miranda wants to name our daughter, it's fine with me."

Chapter 27

Darien's eagerness to learn how to care for Marisa surprised and pleased Miranda. During the course of a congratulatory house call by Shayla, he discovered the mother of two and grandmother of five had owned and operated a child care business back home in Colorado. He asked her to coach him and she obliged.

"He's a natural," Shayla marveled. "Buck never did learn how to diaper our babies. He'd yell 'Woman, you better come here.' He'd turn those little ones every which way but loose trying to get them to burp. Both Timmy and Katy wailed until their Daddy handed them over to me. But your man," she told Miranda, "he's got the touch."

Miranda focused every spare minute and ounce of energy on weight loss and wedding plans. Sam pulled in favors from clients long on need but short on cash to stage an outdoor fiesta with live music, fresh picked sweet corn and Iowa pork for Buck's barbecue grills.

Darien sent his best man three round trip tickets from Newark to Cedar Rapids. "Nathan is counting down the days until he can be back in Iowa," Jack told his brother, "and Beth wants to know if there's anything she can do."

"Tell her to relax," Darien told his brother. "It's a picnic with a ceremony."

"You haven't been briefed on the details, have you?"

Darien laughed. "Not so much. But everything is happening here at the farmhouse. How big can it get?"

The grounds crew arrived three days before the wedding.

"Why do we need these guys?" Darien asked his bride-to-be. "I have a tractor."

"I know you do, love," Miranda replied. "They're taking care of it so you don't have to."

Sounds of light construction woke Darien early the next morning. He wiped sleep from his eyes and stared down in disbelief at the scene in his backyard. "What the hell," he muttered and grabbed his robe. Miranda stopped him at the bottom of the stairs and handed him Marisa.

"The band needs a stage," she explained.

"What happened to blasting Springsteen through the home theater speakers?" he asked.

She smiled and kissed his cheek. "Sam made sure The Boss is on their playlist." She turned on her heel and disappeared through the back door.

"We know who the boss is and it's sure as hell not me," he muttered to the infant in his arms.

Canvas canopies braced by steel popped up in planned formation that afternoon. A small army of men and women unloaded and unfolded rows of folding chairs and long banquet tables.

"Miranda, exactly how many guests did we invite?"

"Everyone in Harmony is family. We don't want to exclude anyone."

"So what are you telling me? Did we invite the whole town?"

"Well, not the whole town."

A phone call from Buck interrupted Darien's next question. "Hey, partner. How many we got coming to the rehearsal dinner tonight?"

"Your guess is as good as mine," he answered and handed the phone to Miranda.

Darien grumbled through his shower and shave. He stood naked in front of his bedroom closet and grunted when Miranda's arms circled his waist from behind.

"So tell me what I'm supposed to wear," he growled.

She peeked around his shoulder and winked. "What you're wearing right now looks good to me."

"Oh, c'mon, Miranda." He pulled away from her and sat down on the bed. "I'm serious."

"You're also grumpy." She sat down next to him and stroked his thigh. He groaned as his penis responded to her touch. "It's been a long time." Her fingertips teased him to full erection. "Too long," she purred. She reached beneath the billowy skirt of her pale yellow sundress and dropped her panties to the floor. Her hands on his shoulders pushed him back on the bed.

She slid him deep inside, surrounding him in wet warmth and erotic sensation. He burrowed beneath the filmy folds of fabric and steered her movements with the grip and release of his hands on her buttocks. She wove her fingers into fists through her hair and moaned through parted lips to high-pitched rapture. He moved with her, cried out and released a pent up flood into her.

She rolled away and against him in sweet, soft afterglow embrace. "Feeling better?" she asked.

He laughed. "Much." He kissed her. Long, slow, deep, luxurious moments of love shared. "I love you," he whispered.

"That's good because I love you and we're getting married in less than 24 hours." She swung her legs over the side of the bed and pulled her sundress over her head. "Get dressed. I'm wearing jeans." She leaned across him and her breasts brushed his chest. "The minister will be here in an hour." She kissed him, stood and headed down the hallway. He heard water hit the shower walls.

"Minister?" he asked aloud and got up to shower again.

Sam and Miranda sat at the kitchen table, talking in hushed tones. Half the buttons on Miranda's short-sleeved sky blue blouse were undone to nurse Marisa.

"Jack just called," Miranda confirmed. "They're on their way. They should be here any minute."

Darien halted his descent from the second floor at the mention of his brother's name.

"Is everything ready?" he heard Miranda say.

"Checked and double checked." Sam said. She giggled. "This is so awesome! I can't wait to see the look on Darien's face."

"More surprises?" The startled women looked up. Darien tried to scowl but grinned in spite of himself.

Miranda handed the sleeping baby to her sister and buttoned her blouse. "I think I saw the minister's car pull into the driveway." She got up and opened the front door.

"Yeah, about that," Darien said. He followed her onto the front porch. "Why is this minister driving a 12 passenger van?"

Jack hopped out of the driver's seat and slammed the van door. "Hey, Iowa!" Beth exited the front passenger's side, waved, and slid open the door behind hers. Nathan jumped out, yelled "Uncle D!" and reached in to help other passengers.

Stewart gripped his grandson's arm and got out of the van first. With his feet firmly planted, he took his wife's hand and assisted Nathan in helping Donna out of the vehicle without incident.

"Mom. Dad." Dazed Darien walked the driveway toward his elderly parents, stunned that they had made the trip. The appearance of two more apparitions from the back of the van quickened his steps.

"Greetings from the land down under!" Evan stuck out his hand to Darien. Hannah bear hugged her uncle.

Darien wrapped his arm around their necks, pulled each of them close, and held on to his family for countless precious and fleeting moments in a lifetime.

The young pastor unfolded long, lean, legs covered in black jeans from the driver's side well of his aging MG Midget. The perfect white teeth in his smile matched the starched white collar under his dimpled chin.

"Good evening, all. Pastor Chad Davis," he said, offered his hand to the men and a friendly hug for the women. "Are we ready to get started?"

"Are you a minister?" Darien's mother asked him.

"Yes, ma'am. I've served the faithful of Our Savior Lutheran Church here in Harmony for six years now."

She smiled and patted Darien's hand. "He's a minister," she said, obviously pleased that this time, unlike the first ceremony, a man of the cloth would preside at her son's wedding.

Hannah held Marisa while the bridal party followed Pastor Chad's rehearsal instructions. Beth offered to take the baby from her daughter. But Hannah continued to rock from side to side, shifting her weight from one foot to the other. "That's OK. I don't mind," she said and cuddled the baby closer.

Darien, Jack and Nathan unloaded half the luggage from the van into the farmhouse. Jack and Beth took the upstairs guest room and Nathan tossed his soft-sided bag and bedroll onto the back porch. Sam drove Darien's parents and Hannah and her husband to the three-bedroom McCullough family home in Harmony where her guests would stay.

"Are you sure this isn't a bother, dear?" Donna asked Sam.

Sam reassured Darien's mother with an impulsive hug and kiss on the cheek. "Not in the least. We're family."

The sign on the diner's door at Hank's Longhorn Café read "Closed for the Wedding." Buck and Shayla welcomed the bridal party with open arms and a roast beef dinner served on red and white checkered tablecloths.

"Beef tonight and Iowa pork tomorrow," Buck said.

"My compliments to the chef," Darien praised.

Buck grinned and nodded. "Much obliged."

Shayla served up flaky crust cherry pie topped with homemade vanilla ice cream. "There'll be more where that came from at the reception," she said and everyone applauded.

"Do you need any help tomorrow?" Darien asked Buck. "I'm pretty sure Miranda went door-to-door with invitations."

Buck threw back his lion mane-like head and roared with laughter. "Tomorrow is your day and hers, my friend. My grilling buddies and me and Shayla and her church ladies have got it covered. We'll do you proud."

Chapter 28

Darien got up as usual at dawn, brought the baby to Miranda, and lay down beside them to enjoy the calm. Preparations below invaded his dreamless sleep hours later.

"Aw, shit," he cursed at the clock. He grabbed his robe, stepped into slippers, and walked downstairs into a perking hub of activity. His brother rescued him with a cup of coffee and a heaping plate of donuts.

"Men only on the back porch," Jack said.

Darien chose a glazed pastry and settled on the cushion in a wicker chair between his father and Evan. "Where's Nathan?" he asked.

Stewart gestured beyond the orchard. "Out there with Ivory."

The donuts disappeared and preparations for the wedding festivities unfolded before their eyes. Buck and several large men in full length white aprons maneuvered grills, propane canisters and coolers. Shayla led the parade of church ladies relaying wave after wave of pans and dishes covered in tin foil.

"Sure is a world away from the rooftop in Brooklyn," Jack observed.

"Reminds me of the Australian outback," Evan commented.

"Iowa isn't as flat as I thought it would be," Stewart said. "This is a fine piece of property you have here, son. Good place to raise a family."

Darien shook his head. "If anyone had told me I was going to own 14 acres and a farmhouse in Iowa, marry a small-town girl and have a baby daughter, I would have asked them what the hell they'd been smoking."

"You could have done a lot worse," Jack said. "Miranda is a beautiful woman and your daughter looks just like you."

"So I've heard and noticed," Darien said.

"You're outnumbered now," Jack remarked. "But maybe you'll get lucky like I did and the next baby will be a boy."

"I'm not sure there will be a next baby."

"Why not?" asked Jack.

"Miranda went through hell having this one."

Stewart grunted. "Once a woman has a child, she'll want another."

Darien stared at his father and turned to his brother, who nodded in agreement.

"Hannah and I discussed this topic at great length before we got married," Evan chimed in.

228

"And?" asked Jack.

"We agreed to wait until we were financially secure and settled in our careers before we start a family."

Stewart shifted in the wicker chair. "Hannah has spent a lot of time taking care of Marisa."

"Hannah likes to be helpful. That's the way she is," Evan responded.

"Oh, it's more than that," Jack said. "Beth has offered to take Marisa. But Hannah just goes right on bouncing and rocking the baby."

Evan opened his mouth in wordless protest. Stewart's advice broke the semi-awkward silence. "Better keep a gross of rubbers handy," he told him.

His sons laughed until their sides ached.

Beth and Donna herded the men upstairs at noon. Jokes exchanged as each showered, shaved and dressed for the wedding reached fraternity party levels of laughter when each appeared in the hallway wearing tan slacks and white shirts.

"All we need is an ice cream truck," Jack remarked.

Beth climbed the stairs and frowned at the foursome. "Oh, for heaven's sake." She marched to the room she and her husband were sharing and handed him a sea glass green shirt. "This comes closest to matching the color of Sam's dress." She turned to her son-in-law. "I don't suppose you brought anything else with you."

"Sorry," he muttered and shoved his hands in his pants pockets.

Beth sighed. "Dad, you and Darien are the same size. Let's go raid his closet." She chose a sky blue shirt for Stewart and handed Darien another in cream-colored linen. "Get changed. The ceremony starts in 10 minutes."

"Yes ma'am," Darien said and kissed her cheek.

Final preparations passed in a flurry of bouquets, boutonnieres and corsages arriving in the Range Rover with the bride and her maid of honor. New neighbor Trevor separated himself from the aisles of guests to open the car door, take Sam's arm and help her safely navigate the terrain in her ankle-length gown and pumps. Jack intercepted Darien before he did the same for Miranda.

"You know the rules," Jack said and hustled his brother down the aisle to stand beside Pastor Chad.

Darien scanned the front row of guests. Evan glanced nervously at Hannah cuddling Marisa. Nathan gave him the thumbs-up from his seat between his mother and grandmother. The folding chair next to Donna on the aisle was empty. The band's keyboardist played the opening chords of the Bridal March. Sam began walking toward them. "Where's Dad?" Darien whispered to Jack.

"Right there," he said and nodded down the aisle.

Darien's breath caught in his throat and he blinked back tears. Stewart had stepped in as father of his radiant bride.

The afternoon celebration continued through sunset under azure skies dotted and streaked with passing puffs of white. The ebb and flow of guests consumed pounds of barbequed pork chops, sweet corn grilled in husks peeled back and dipped in melted butter, vats of potato salad and coleslaw and a multi-tiered white wedding cake. Beer kegs were tapped and emptied, bartenders poured cases of wine and children consumed cans of chilled soda pop.

Darien and Jack kicked back with beers on the screened-in porch four hours after the exchange of vows and rings.

"Man, what a feast," Jack said and patted his stomach. "I'm glad I stopped at four pork chops."

"Yeah, it's been quite a day."

Jack caught the wavering tone in his brother's voice. "OK, tell me what you're thinking, D."

Darien drank his beer and stared out at the party on his property. "This is what Ali wanted for our wedding. You remember her cousin, Patrice?"

"Yeah, she was Ali's matron of honor."

"Ali told me about Patrice and Dan's wedding at home on their lawn. Just like this." His eyes misted over. Jack felt the iron grip of melancholy descending on his brother as on the dreadful day of Ali's funeral.

"Hey, man, don't go there." He scooted the wicker chair closer, punched Darien's arm and nodded toward a laughing Miranda. A circle of peaches and cream flowers tied with blue ribbon adorned the crown of copper hair that cascaded down the back of her pale peach wedding gown. She turned and smiled at her husband. "That lovely lady is your wife now. Live in the now, D."

The leader of the band stepped up to the microphone and picked up a guitar. "I've just been reminded that the bride and groom haven't danced together yet." The young musician who'd caught and held the attention of several single ladies in the crowd slung the strap over his shoulder, grinned and pointed at Darien. "You all probably know Darien was just passing through Harmony. Then he got a look at our Miranda and the road trip was over." Laughter, applause and chants of "Get out here and dance with your wife" coaxed a red-faced Darien from the back porch to stand beside his bride.

"Miranda said we could play whatever we want. So we came up with a tune by the Traveling Wilburys." He stepped back, tapped his foot and called out to his band "End of the Line, two, three, four," and began to strum and sing.

Darien took Miranda's hand and twirled her under his arm. The shuffling joy of the upbeat melody brought hands together and every guest that could to their feet. "Kiss her!" they shouted after the last note. Darien pulled his bride close, pressed his lips to hers, and forgot the past in the joy of the moment.

Chapter 29

Restlessness nagged Darien, especially during the long late summer afternoons while the baby slept. Sam had hired an office manager replacement for Miranda before Marisa's birth. The retired widow needed the job and Miranda was only too happy to spend mornings with her family. After lunch and nursing Marisa before naptime, Miranda would leave to open her studio in Harmony.

With no projects to complete or prospects to pursue, the rural quiet roared in Darien's ears. An unexpected phone call offered relief.

"Is this Chef Darien McKenna?" the unfamiliar female voice asked.

"Speaking," he answered.

"Do you know Trevor Grady?"

My sister-in-law sure does, he thought. He grinned. "Yes, he's a family friend."

"This is Amanda Jennings. I'm the director of the culinary arts program at the community college in Cedar Rapids. My husband works with Trevor. He gave me your phone number and recommended I call you about an open adjunct faculty position."

"That's very kind of him. But I don't have the credentials to teach."

"Trevor told Jerry that you were an executive chef in Manhattan."

"That's true. But I didn't go to college."

"The state of Iowa does not require trades and technical instructors at community colleges to have a degree. Professional experience is valued very highly and from what I understand you earned a Michelin star. We would be honored if you would consider joining us."

"I'm flattered, really I am. But I'm not a teacher."

"Tell me, how many years did you run a kitchen?"

He laughed. "I don't know. Maybe 20."

"And in all those years you never had to teach a skill to anyone?"

"You got me there. Of course I did."

"I'll be honest with you. We are really in a bind here. The chef who was scheduled to begin teaching two sections of an advanced food prep class next week with 30 students enrolled in each class cancelled out on us. Will you at least accept an invitation to meet and take a tour of the campus and the kitchens?"

The quiet weighed on him. His decision lifted him. "Where, when and what time?" he asked.

Miranda stirred chili bubbling in a pot over the stove burner flame. Darien wrapped his arms around her waist and nibbled her neck.

She giggled. "Open flame," she warned and poked a wooden spoon of thick red broth at his lips.

"Mmmm," he hummed, "hard to say which tastes better."

"You're in a good mood." She set the spoon in its silver rest and turned down the flame to simmer. "The interview must have gone well."

"It did." He set the table as he talked. "The kitchens are very well equipped and the lesson plan didn't scare me off."

"What about the people?" Miranda asked.

"Amanda is all business, very professional. The office staff is friendly and the other instructors couldn't wait to ask me questions and pick my brain."

Miranda filled tall glasses with ice water, scooped chili into bowls and sat across the table from her husband. "So, are you going to take the job?"

He smiled at her. "I already did."

"Good," she said and spread her napkin on her lap. "I have my art. You need this."

Later that evening, after his wife and daughter had gone to bed, Darien punched his cellphone speed dial connection to New Jersey.

"Jack? You're not going to believe this. I'm a teacher."

Darien stuffed a pile of exams in the brown leather briefcase he'd purchased to shuttle itinerant necessities from home to classroom. He greeted the pastry chef preparing to take over the kitchen and walked into the hallway teeming with students and staff.

"Chef?" Darien recognized the approaching baby-faced young man as Mike Pratt, a promising third year student who seemed to absorb skills like a thick and thirsty side towel. "Where were you exec in Manhattan?"

"Chez Nous," Darien replied.

"Upper west side?"

Darien smiled. "That's right. Have you been?"

Mike shook his head. "No, but my cousin is an apprentice to a chef in Midtown. He's scoped out most of the restaurants in Manhattan and said Chez Nous is one of the best. When I told him I was taking a class from you, he called me a liar."

Darien laughed. "Tell him if he doesn't believe you to ask Eric. He was my sous chef. He owns Chez Nous."

Their conversation continued through the doors and into the faculty parking lot. Mike's good-natured envy of his cousin's life in the big city triggered repressed homesickness as images of days past consumed Darien's thoughts.

"Tom is really psyched about a charity gig he's working. Bid Against Hunger. Have you heard of it, Chef?"

Darien leaned against his car and closed his eyes. He saw delicate fingers on a petite hand reach for crostini, ricotta and Italian sausage. Her chocolate brown eyes sparkled again and he yearned for the lovely lady in red as she vanished into the glitz and glam of the gala evening.

"Chef?" Mike's voice forced him back. "Are you OK?"

He straightened and opened the door behind the driver's side. "I'm fine." He tossed the briefcase on the seat and slammed the door. "Yes, I'm familiar with the event. I worked it once."

Mike's eyes went wide. "Cool. What did you serve?"

"Bruschetta."

"Do you still have the recipe? Can we make it in class?"

Darien got in and started the engine. "I'll think about it," he answered. "See you tomorrow."

The golden light of fall bathed the changing colors of Iowa foliage day after predictable day, keeping Darien grounded in the now of his life. But the past haunted his night time hours. In deep sleep, he commanded the kitchen at Chez Nous, took the subway home to Brooklyn, shared a newspaper in the morning and a bottle of wine at night with Ali, and breathed in the lilac scent of her in as she slept in his arms. He'd reach for her in the morning and felt guilty about dreams he could not control when reality dawned and she was gone, replaced by Miranda.

Miranda spent limited hours in her Harmony studio as the stream of tourists interested in purchasing artwork slowed to a trickle. Still, he was surprised when she came home early on a Saturday afternoon. She stood in the doorway to the nursery, her hands on her hips and a pout on her lips.

"Everything OK, sweetheart?" He held their sleeping daughter against his chest and continued the slow, steady motion of the big oak rocking chair.

She sighed. "I wish I could answer yes."

He frowned in concern. "What's wrong?"

"I don't know. You tell me."

Uh, oh, he thought. Think before you speak, D.

"I don't know what to say. Is there something you need, love?"

"My husband."

"I'm right here."

"Are you? Darien, I'm truly glad you're a good father to Marisa. But what about us? You've been going through the motions for weeks. And I get the feeling you're not really here. You're somewhere else wishing you were with someone else. So what I need to know is do you want to be with me?" She backed out and into the hallway. "Let me know what you decide." He heard her ballet flats slap the floor and the door to her home studio click closed.

Busted! he thought. "Damn it," he muttered under his breath, "another woman who can read my mind." He got up, settled his baby girl in her crib, and covered her with a petal soft pink blanket.

He gazed out the window over the fields of spent corn and the vanishing afternoon sun shifting shadows cast on his front lawn. He struggled to understand himself. An answer eluded him even as he turned the knob on the door to the room next to the nursery.

She sat on a stool in the center of her studio and leaned toward a mostly blank canvas perched on an easel. Sunlight poured through the panes of tall bare windows set in eggshell white walls to the left and right of the corner she faced. The high polish of hardwood that surrounded her enhanced the sheen of natural illumination. She'd tied her mane of glowing copper-colored hair back with a royal purple ribbon that matched laces over the bodice and tied at the wrists on the sleeves of her blouse. Its translucent fabric clung to her, teasing him hard with suggested sensuality. The denim skirt hugged her long bare legs at mid-thigh. She dipped a brush into paint squeezed from a tube, filled tips of soft bristles with traffic signal green, and altered the canvas to reflect her creative vision.

What the hell is wrong with you? the voice in his head scolded. *This sexy, gorgeous woman is your wife. BE HER HUSBAND!*

He walked toward her. She glanced up at him.

"Don't mind me," he encouraged her. She turned back to the canvas and dipped the brush again.

He stood behind her and watched her work. "You've switched to acrylics."

"The colors are truer." She swirled the paint to a rolling arc of distant horizon.

"Business or pleasure?" he asked.

"Both, I hope. Pleasure for now."

He waited until she lifted the brush from the canvas sat upright on the stool. He leaned into her, breathed her in. His fingers kneaded muscled knots in her neck and shoulders. She moaned, closed her eyes, and let her head drop back against him. "That feels nice," she whispered.

"What color are you seeing now?" he asked.

"Yellow."

"Then paint it."

She selected another brush and washed a thin layer of diluted yellow paint above the green horizon. He coaxed the bodice ribbon open, caressed her soft contours and cupped her breasts in his hands. She dipped the brush again and stroked pure gold onto the canvas.

"Why the bright shade?" he asked.

"For caution. The light is changing."

He bent and kissed her below each ear. "So is the position." He stepped around the stool, squatted and sat on his heels in the space between her and the easel. He kissed the insides of her knees and explored her thighs with the tip of his tongue as far as the hem of the denim skirt would allow. His fingers reached in and pushed aside her panties, stirring the juices he desired. "I need a little help here, sweetheart."

She dipped her brush in the palette's brightest color and slashed it across the canvas. His eyes caught her movements and he questioned the meaning.

"Red," he said. "Do you want me to stop?"

She dropped the brush, rose from the stool, pulled her skirt over her hips and let him slip her panties off and to the floor. "Keep going," she implored and perched on the edge of the stool.

"Keep painting," he said and opened her legs wide.

He slid his fingers deep inside her and felt her quiver. "Still red?"

She drew a shaky breath. "Deep red."

His thumb circled the engorged, twitching spot. "How about now?"

"Cotton candy pink."

"Let me taste it." His lips closed over her. His tongue plunged inside, probing, stimulating her arousal to climax. He covered her parted lips with his hand to muffle moans that might wake their baby.

She pulled at his belt. "Take them off. It's my turn." He stood in front of her, peeled off trousers and briefs. He groaned when her lips surrounded him and the tip of his penis touched the back of her throat. Her fingers stroked his genitals softly, like delicate bristles on a paintbrush. Brilliant hues of color in his world splashed, swirled and exploded with the force of his release.

She sat back on the stool and grinned up at him. "What color did you see?" she asked.

"The entire spectrum of the rainbow." He took her hand, led her to their bed, and removed the last of the clothing that covered them. He stood over her, admired her beauty, caressed every inch of her until she opened herself and invited him in. He took her slowly, sweetly, lovingly, patiently, held on until he felt her join with him completely. Colors flashed, blurred and softened and they dozed, content in the satisfied warmth of afterglow.

Marisa's cry woke her parents. Darien rose, wrapped in a robe, and brought the baby to Miranda. He tucked the comforter around them, kissed his wife and the infant she nursed. The perfection of the moment and the strength of the love he felt for them overwhelmed and empowered him. His heart leapt at the possibility that the love they'd made that afternoon had conceived a second child.

Later that night in their bed and bedroom bathed in full moonlight, Darien gave Miranda her answer. "I'm here with you and that's where I want to be," he said.

She kissed him and snuggled closer. "There's only one thing that could make me happier than I am right now."

"Anything you want, my love."

"I want another baby."

He laughed and held her tight against him.

"What's so funny?"

"My Dad and Jack told me you would. What's funny is I do, too." He rolled to top her and parted her legs with his knee. "Let's see what we can do about that."

Fall dissolved to winter in a flurry of harvest, Thanksgiving and the first dusting of snow. The extended Harmony family of neighbors repaid the McKenna's invitation to pick the orchard's apples with gifts of homemade jelly and jam, canned mincemeat and cinnamon-spiced applesauce. Packages arrived from New Jersey the week before Christmas with gifts for the couple and their baby's first Christmas. Darien protested but gave in to Miranda's pleas and plans for an outing through knee-deep snow to find the perfect tree in the woods. He slogged with a handsaw and rope, retrieved and transported the 8-foot-tall pine strapped to the Range Rover's roof. The holiday symbol stood tall and proud, aglow with lights and laden with ornaments and tinsel in the corner of their front room. Stockings embroidered with the names Darien, Miranda, Marisa and Ivory hung from the fireplace mantle.

The phone's ring and shouts of delight woke Darien early on Christmas morning. Marisa gurgled and giggled in her mother's arms as Miranda whirled and danced around the bedroom. "Trevor proposed to Sam! My little sister is getting married!" The Christmas dinner tabled bathed in candlelight provided the perfect setting for Sam to show off her shimmering diamond solitaire ring. The newly-engaged couple shared infectious smiles of joy and a wedding date in early June.

Darien and Ivory returned from their evening patrol of the property on New Year's Eve to find an unexpected guest begging table scraps from Miranda.

"Why is Dave ringing in the New Year with us?" Darien asked her.

"Sam and Trevor are at a party in Cedar Rapids. They're spending the night in a fancy hotel suite reserved and paid for by Trevor's employer."

Darien scratched the Malamute's ears and kissed his wife. "I should warn Trevor. McCullough women are fertile." He lifted a corner of plastic wrap from the plate on the counter and reached for a leftover hunk of ham. Miranda playfully slapped his hand.

"Apparently, so are you." His mouth dropped open and she fed him the ham. "Happy new life, Daddy."

Darien watched snow fall on the rural Iowa winter landscape from the comfort of his couch and a room warmed by bio-fuel flames in the fireplace. His wife and daughter were nestled in beds above him. His dog slept in a Husky wrapped circle at his feet, her nose under a bushy white tail.

He looked at his wristwatch. The ball was about to drop at Times Square. He reached for his cellphone and speed dialed New Jersey.

"Happy New Year, Jack."

"Same to you, man. How's the family?"

"About to get bigger."

"No kidding? Pun totally intended. So when's baby number two due?"

"On our first wedding anniversary."

"I'll be a grandfather before then."

Darien laughed. "Well, I guess Evan didn't take Dad's advice."

"Apparently not. Hannah is thrilled and Beth is already checking flight schedules."

Darien heard the familiar countdown broadcast in the background. "You better get off the phone and kiss your wife."

"Yeah, you do the same. Congratulations, D."

"Same to you, Grandpa."

He closed the connection to the East Coast and let his mind wander back one last time to another New Year's Eve. Snow falling on the Brooklyn Bridge. Lilacs and silk.

"New Year, a new life," she'd said.

He touched his fingers to his lips and raised an imaginary glass of champagne to heaven. "Here's to both, Ali my love."

Darien rubbed Ivory's ears and flicked the wall switch to extinguish the fireplace flame. He climbed the stairs, leaned over the crib, and hummed a lullaby to his sleeping daughter. He dropped the last clothes worn in the old year in the bathroom hamper and slid into bed beside Miranda.

She yawned. "Is it midnight?"

"Almost." He snuggled up against her warmth and kissed his pregnant wife.

"Happy New Year, my love."

*The saga concludes in **Belonging***

**When Marisa's certain path to her future ends, the
struggle to recover from heartbreak begins.**
Darien's daughter admires and adores her Michelin
star chef father. Lessons learned at his side earn her
acceptance into a prestigious school of culinary arts and an
apprenticeship at the upscale Midtown Manhattan kitchen
he once commanded. Pressure to succeed crushes her
confidence. Devastating loss shatters her world. Marisa's
search to find a new path leads to the land of the McKenna
Clan and the arms of a heart-stopping handsome, yet
lonely man.

New Life in Love Trilogy
Reservations Heartland Belonging
Tales from Heartland
Four Short Stories and Love Unlikely novella

*"I read the entire trilogy, becoming impatient waiting for
the 2nd and then 3rd books to come out! The author doesn't
follow a formula, but rather the characters' lives unfold
in some predictable and very unpredictable ways. I love
LaBella's style and will continue to follow her works."*

Teresa LaBella has been fascinated with fiction since she learned to read. Professional years invested learning the craft of writing and the art of storytelling as a journalist, grant writer and consultant pushed the author past the fiction writing stage of idea to 'I did' in the New Life in Love contemporary romance series.

Teresa and her Canadian filmmaker husband John LaBella are at home with their rescue husky fur babies Rosie and Ellis in rural Nova Scotia.

Dear Readers,

The genre writing rule broken in **Heartland** shifted the trilogy away from pure romance to the McKenna family saga that began as a sweet and simple love story in **Reservations**.

Darien's sudden and tragic loss closes one book and begins another New Life in Love with Miranda. Their story set in Harmony introduces readers to short story **Tales From Heartland** and the next generation of the McKenna Clan – Marisa's quest to find her place of **Belonging** in the third book of the trilogy and Rachel's healing through **Love Unlikely,** the novella.

I'm pleased to share these stories with you. No matter which you choose to read, recommendations to book clubs, co workers, family and friends and reviews on Goodreads and/or Amazon are the best way to help others discover a book you enjoyed. Thank you!

I love to connect with my readers!

Visit my website www.storyteller30.com

Facebook.com/storyteller30

Twitter @teresalabella